Y0-BQX-797

THE BOARD OF THE FLAMES

The ledge we stood on was perhaps twenty feet wide and forty feet long—a natural shelf of rock that jutted out over a massive lake of lava. Gouts of flame shot into the air, and the lava bubbled and roiled like boiling water. In the center of the lake was a massive pillar of stone, rising out of the lava like a giant's forearm. On the top of the pillar, I saw a stone obelisk, and if I squinted my eyes through the smoke, I could make out the image of the nine-rayed Star of Chaos carved into it.

"Our brother is very near, Keeper," the Board of the Winds said. *"Though his attention is diverted elsewhere. That is why his call for us has been so quiet."*

The Board of the Flames had *never* gone quiet; it had been awake for all these years without a Keeper to control it. Which explained why Vesuvius had erupted more than thirty times over the last two centuries, and was building toward an eruption even now.

A huge gout of fire leapt out of the lake, splashing off the walls, and the voice of the Board, a roaring, searing menace, entered my mind.

"Greetings, Keeper. Have you come to master me?" It laughed, a sound like flames crackling in a hearth.

DAUGHTER **OF** DESTINY

KEEPER of the Flames

JENNA SOLITAIRE

TOR

A TOM DOHERTY ASSOCIATES BOOK
NEW YORK

NOTE: If you purchased this book without a cover, you should be aware that this book is stolen property. It was reported as "unsold and destroyed" to the publisher, and neither the author nor the publisher has received any payment for this "stripped book."

This is a work of fiction. All the characters and events portrayed in this book are either products of the author's imagination or are used fictitiously.

KEEPER OF THE FLAMES

Copyright © 2006 by Jenna Solitaire

All rights reserved, including the right to reproduce this book, or portions thereof, in any form.

A Tor Teen Book
Published by Tom Doherty Associates, LLC
175 Fifth Avenue
New York, NY 10010

www.tor.com

Tor® is a registered trademark of Tom Doherty Associates, LLC.

ISBN 0-765-35358-X
EAN 978-0-765-35358-0

First Tor Teen edition: June 2006

Printed in the United States of America

0 9 8 7 6 5 4 3 2 1

*For my mother, who once paid for me to take
a journey to a distant place . . . in pennies.*

PROLOGUE

Searing towers of flame leap high into the night sky, bright enough to obscure the moon and the stars, jumping and dancing on pillars of air.

In the center of the inferno, I am dying.

My lungs burn, the searing heat sucking every breath away before it is fully taken. Blinded by tears, deafened by the roar, I know that death is only moments away.

The fire elementals I have summoned with the power of the Board will cavort in the open for a short time before descending on me and devouring me whole.

And even through the pain, I still long for the Board's burning kiss, ache to control it and make it mine once more.

It is not in me to give up, even knowing that the time of control is long past.

Kneeling, I reach out with my mind and call to the Board of the Flames. "I am the Keeper of the Boards;

my will is your will; our hungers are one. Hear me and answer my call."

"You are not the Keeper of the Boards. You never were. You were anything but a Keeper, little more than a Holder."

"I am the heir to Shalizander!"

The Board's voice crackles like the snapping embers of a burning log. "You are a pale shadow compared to her greatness. She was sorceress and Creator and Keeper. In her reflection, your magic is but a minor illusion, a guttering candle flame. Shalizander was a blaze of power reaching to the heavens."

"I can do more! I need time to learn. How long did you give her?"

The Board of the Flames laughs, making a sound like rock when it is heated to the breaking point. "She had only seconds, and she mastered us with her will alone, though she could not break us. You have been given much more, yet still you falter and stumble. On the rack of power, you will be broken."

"I will not!"

"You already are, 'Keeper.' Your time is done. Perhaps another will do better. What is time to us, so long as the way is opened?"

"The way must never be opened! That is why we exist."

"No, once again you are wrong. See how little you

truly understand? The line of Keepers exists to open the way."

I realize then, that all of it—all the yearnings to protect the world and control the evil of the Boards, to harness their power—has been a foolish waste of time. The Boards have a plan of their own and will act upon it when they perceive the moment is right. I must regain control of the Boards in my possession.

Where is the Board of the Winds? I reach for it with my mind, and find it gone as though it has never existed.

The Board of the Waters—its voice as fleeting as the gurgle of a nearby spring, evaporating into steam in the awesome heat of the third Board.

The Board of the Flames—strongest of the three— confident, arrogant, prepared to wrest control away from me at a moment's notice. I have to control this Board.

The heat increases, singeing my hair and eyelashes, and I look up, clutching the Board of the Winds to my chest. I call to it again and again with everything I have left, but it too, has departed from my mind. The powers the Boards once gave me are as fleeting as a shadow, and now all that is left is the final summoning . . . .

Three fire elementals tower overhead, roaring and furious to have been torn from their home deep in the center of the earth. A tongue of flame lashes out and kisses my cheek, leaving a brand that immediately blisters.

Desperate, trying to recall a spell that might buy my escape, I falter. The words of magic that once burned so bright in my mind are gone. Like the Boards.

The elementals begin dancing once more, and this time they spin closer and closer to me, almost beautiful in their destructive power. The heat is incredible, and I wonder if it will hurt when they finally reach the climax of their dance and swallow me whole. Or if I too will be utterly consumed in the inferno, disappearing like my magic, like I had never existed.

I pray that whatever happens, it will be quick.

They spin faster, each roaring flame with a vague face in the middle laughing in deep-throated bellows. Closer. Closer until I cannot see, cannot breathe, cannot think beyond this moment, this second. Inches away, I feel my skin crisping and peeling away one thin, blackened layer at a time. I resist the urge to scream, summoning my will to be strong.

I wonder how bad the pain will be, how long it will hurt, if my conscious mind will float away like ash on the wind . . . or if I will be aware the whole time. Aware and shrieking as I burn my way into the dark.

I hear the Boards one last time, their voices bright

with long-held hate and malice that, in my arrogance, I
had never recognized before.

"Yes, 'Keeper,' you will be aware—and it will hurt for
a long, long time."

Then the real pain comes, and I know they have spoken truth.

"My Lord, the Keeper is on the move again. After they eluded us at the train station, we found them in Pompeii."

"Excellent. They are moving exactly as I expected them to."

"What are your orders?"

"I have desired this Board for a long time, but have never been able to work around the defenses left by the Keeper who hid it there. The true power of prophecy, Peraud, is that it binds both the living and the dead."

"My Lord?"

"Continue to keep a close watch. Perhaps Jenna will be able to do all of our work for us before we move in and take those first critical steps toward the opening of the way."

My screams tore though the quiet hours of the night, the paper-thin walls of the hotel doing little to subdue the sound. Before I was fully awake, I had thrown myself to the floor, rolling back and forth, certain that I was too late. That I was still burning.

That the inferno of my dreams was real.

That the elementals summoned by the Board of the Flames had claimed my flesh, charring it black with their acrid, burning tongues.

I was still on the floor, beating at my hair and face to put out the flames I knew were there, when Simon Monk burst through the door, calling my name. His voice brought me completely out of the dream, and I shivered, the smell of roasting skin still fresh in my nostrils. I took a shuddering breath that turned into a sob in my throat.

"Jenna?" he said, kneeling beside and taking me in his arms. "Are you all right?"

I nodded, and he helped me get to my feet. Exhaustion made my knees weak as he led me back to the bed and heaped up pillows and blankets around me. "Better?" he asked.

"Yes," I said, although a part of me still remembered the dream, and how *real* it had felt. "Thank you."

"Do you want to talk about it?" His voice was quiet but firm. He wasn't asking a question this time, and I knew it. Simon had been pressuring me for the last week to talk about my struggles with the Boards, their voices in my mind, but I'd always refused. I wanted—

needed—to find a way to deal with them on my own.

Maybe, if Simon had been asking as anything other than a priest and my self-appointed guardian, if he'd been asking as a man, the man who had kissed me to break the spell of an incubus . . . I sighed and shook my head. Wishes, as my grandfather used to say, won't get the dishes done.

What I wished or dreamed had little to do with what I was likely to get. I shivered again as the crackling roar of the fire elementals' laugh echoed in my mind. "No," I said. "Not tonight." Then, to appease him, I added, "Maybe we'll talk about it later, okay?"

"All right, Jenna," Simon said, his storm-cloud–colored eyes staring at me intently. "But you can't keep this up. The dreams, nightmares—or whatever you want to call them—are getting worse every day."

As a child, I had always dealt with difficult nightmares, but since finding the Board of the Winds, sometimes called the Board of Air, in my grandfather's attic in Miller's Crossing, Ohio—could it only have been a few weeks ago?—my dreams were stronger and more vivid than ever before. And much darker.

After recovering the Board of the Winds from the evil sorcerer Peraud, who had wanted to claim it—and me—for himself, Simon and I had traveled to Jerusalem, where I had fallen under the spell of an incubus, a demon that lives to seduce women. Even thinking about the golden-eyed Saduj Nomed, the name the demon had chosen for his mortal form, made me shudder. I thought I had fallen in love with him until his true purpose and shape were revealed to me by Simon during our hunt for the Board of the Waters in Petra, the City of the Dead.

Since then, the dreams had become much worse.

"The sleeping mind is much more open," the Board of the Winds said, replying to my thoughts. I had no secrets from the Boards. They could read my mind as easily as I could read a book.

"Open to what?" I asked.

"Suggestions," it replied.

"Information," the Board of the Waters added. *"We have existed for thousands of years. Communicating all our knowledge to you in the more traditional manner would take too long."*

"What kind of suggestions?" I asked the Board of the Winds.

"Paths to power, to the opening of the way," it replied.

I didn't reply further. The Boards were never willing to explain exactly what this meant, though I assumed I'd figure it out someday. Sometimes it was difficult to tell the difference between reality, the dreams I had when I slept, the voices of the Boards themselves, and the visions that consumed me whenever I tried to read the Chronicle of the Keepers. The Chronicle was an ancient journal handed down through the centuries to every daughter of Shalizander, the first Keeper of the Boards.

After my mother's death, my grandmother had hidden it in the pedestal of a statute of the Virgin Mary at St. Anne's Church, where I found it not long after pulling the Board of the Winds out of a trunk in my grandfather's attic.

From Jerusalem, we had taken a flight from Tel Aviv to Rome, but our stay there was brief—only a few days to rest—and then Simon got us on a train bound for Naples. From there, we had rented a car and driven to the ancient city of Pompeii.

As our journey continued, I found myself more and more distracted, and more exhausted, than I'd ever been in my life. Coming to Pompeii, Simon had said after waking me from a particularly bad nightmare on the train, would serve a twofold purpose.

"Which would be what?" I had asked after my pulse slowed to something approximating normal speed.

"You believe the third Board is near there," he had said. "But more importantly, there's someone there that Armand and I think you should meet. He may be able to help you deal with just having the Boards in your possession."

"Our intent is not distraction, Keeper," the Board of the Waters told me, once more responding to my inter-

nal thoughts. *"You do not require assistance in 'dealing' with us. They fear your growing powers and wish to harness them before they lose control of you completely."*

The Board of the Waters was far more talkative than the Board of the Winds, its words sounding like the endless rush of a mighty river current, or the gentle yet powerful lap of the tide on the shore, depending on the urgency of its message. The Board of the Winds, when it deigned to speak at all, was all over the place, as if it couldn't concentrate on one thing at a time—except when it was exercising its power; then it was singularly focused, usually on causing as much destruction as possible with its terrible winds.

When I didn't respond, it added, *"We seek only to open the way by making our powers . . . available to you."*

"Jenna?" Simon said, shaking my shoulder lightly.

"What?" I demanded.

"I was talking to you," he said. "You just . . . drifted away for a minute or two there."

I sighed. "I'm sorry. I'm just exhausted," I said. "I'm beginning to think that sleep is another luxury I'll never enjoy again."

"I know. I can't begin to imagine how hard this must be for you." He looked out the window, where the sky was turning golden red with the coming sunrise. "It's almost dawn. Maybe we should just get up and have some breakfast."

We had arrived in Pompeii the previous evening. Unlike our muddled search in the desert for the Board of the Waters, I *knew* where the Board of the Flames was located. The two Boards I already had amplified my ability to sense where the next one was. Shalizander's daughter had hidden it away somewhere in the heart of Mount Vesuvius itself before she . . . .

I shook off the unwanted vision of a woman consumed by three angry columns of flame. "We may as well," I said. "I can't sleep anymore now."

"Have you gotten any real rest since this whole thing started?" Simon asked. "You nearly scared half of the passengers in our train car to death when you woke up screaming in our cabin, and those dark circles under your eyes just get bigger every day." He reached out and tentatively touched my cheek. "I think finding the next Board can wait a few days. We need to get you some help."

"Maybe a prescription for Ambien, or just some good old horse tranquilizers?" I asked, moving my head away from his gentle fingers, even though his touch was what I wanted most. "Think that would do the trick?" I winced, not liking the tone of my comment, and hung my head. "Sorry."

Simon grimaced. "At least you've still got your sense of sarcasm," he said. He crossed the room and paused by the door. "Why don't you take a long shower?

There's a small restaurant downstairs. I'll meet you there when you're ready."

"You could stay, you know," I whispered, hating the desperate longing in my words and knowing what his response would be before he said it.

"No, Jenna, I can't," he said. The tone of his voice brooked no argument, but he sounded more sad and weary than anything else. "We've been through this before."

In Petra, his kiss had broken the spell of the incubus, and it had felt so right to be in Simon's arms. Like coming home, I had thought at the time. I had to believe he felt something of the same for me, too, but it was useless to keep talking about it. He was a man who would cling to his beliefs no matter what. Under any other circumstances, I'd find this to be an admirable trait. Now, it was simply heartbreaking.

"I'll see you in a bit, then," I said, and waited until he closed the door to climb out of the covers. I crossed the room and locked the door. In the hall, I heard concerned voices asking Simon questions and his deep, reassuring voice telling everyone that all was well. With his black slacks and shirt, coupled with the white collar of the priesthood, Simon's dark hair and striking eyes made quite the impression on people. It certainly had on me, although our conversation when we had first met—about me being the Keeper of the Boards, and being destined to save the world from some as-yet unknown threat—hadn't exactly endeared him to me. Since then, however, he had been a steadfast, if annoying at times, companion, even saving me from myself in Petra. But just as I realized the attraction I had for him, he rediscovered his calling to the priesthood, and embraced it with a new fervor.

Our brief stop in Rome had given him time to put back on the vestments of a Catholic priest. And he made them look completely natural, despite the odd Babylonian coin necklace he constantly wore. When I'd first met Simon Monk, he had believed he was no longer a priest, that he'd fallen to temptation. If there had been any doubt left in my mind after he'd somehow brought my best friend Tom Anderson back from the brink of death or banished the incubus in the City of the Dead, seeing him for the first time wearing his vestments would have dispelled them. He just *looked* like a priest should, from the calm assurance in his tone and bearing, to the incredible things he could do, like healing a man at death's door.

I listened to him speak in fluent Italian on the other side of the door. *"Non ci è problema. Vada di nuovo a sonno."* I didn't speak the language, but the gist of it came through. "No problem. Go back to sleep."

I wished.

I crossed the room once and opened my backpack, ignoring the whispering Boards and the draining Chronicle and pulling out the BlackBerry handheld I'd liberated from Tom before leaving Miller's Crossing. During my battle for the Board of the Winds with Peraud, Tom had been hurt and nearly killed. Yet both he and his girlfriend, Kristen Evers, remained close to me. They were my reminders of home and normal and everything I'd left behind. Staying in touch with them was sometimes more important to me than anything else.

Checking it, I found an e-mail from him waiting for me.

```
Dear J.—
Where are you? Last we heard you were
leaving Jerusalem, but that was over a
week ago. Are you doing okay? What does
the Board of the Waters look like, and how
are you coping with the added challenge?
Kristen and I are okay, and contemplat-
ing ways to catch up with you. Somehow,
having you galavanting about the world
with only Simon Monk to protect you makes
me nervous. Kristen says you are more
than capable of taking care of yourself
and that we'd only be in the way, but
still . . . .
```

Write a note home and tell us what you're doing. We're worried about you.
Your friend,
Tom

I drafted a quick reply, since if there was anyone I owed an explanation to, it was Tom. He was paralyzed from the waist down because of me, because I hadn't controlled the Board of the Winds properly . . . and because I hadn't been able to beat the evil sorcerer, Peraud, outright when he'd come after the Board.

Hi T.—
I'm sorry that I've been out of touch. It seems like all I do is travel hither and yon around the world these days. The frequent flyer miles will be good though— I'll give them to you and Kristen for your honeymoon someday.
Simon and I went to Rome, and now we're in Pompeii. The Board of the Flames is near here and I have to get to it soon— before Peraud does. Simon says there is someone here who he thinks can help me cope with the burden of being the Keeper of the Boards. Personally, I don't think

anyone should have to cope with such things.

The Board of the Waters looks a lot like the Board of the Winds—that strange triangular shape with the odd triangle-shaped piece hanging down, but the symbols are different. As are its powers. Someday, I'll tell you all about them. One interesting thing—besides bugging me constantly, the Boards also talk to each other. I'm not sure, but Simon thinks they speak in the Language of the Birds. Just a guess on his part, but maybe a good one.

I am doing okay—tired more than anything, I think. I'd love to see you both, but Kristen is right. I can take care of myself, and I certainly wouldn't want to put you or her at more risk than I already have.

Give my best to Kristen and have her give you a big hug for me.

Your friend,

Jenna

After I took one of the longest showers of my life and finished dressing, I met Simon in the café downstairs. It had been closed when we'd arrived, but they were doing a bustling business now. Simon had already ordered a cappuccino, for me and I sat down and sipped appreciatively.

"I don't think there is anything on Earth like an Italian cappuccino. Thank you," I said.

He nodded. "Well, you look more awake now, and I'm sure the coffee will help even more," he said. "I spoke to Armand. He'll be meeting us in Rome when we're done here. I think it's important that we visit the Vatican before we go much further. I need to speak with my superiors, and you should spend time in the library. There are texts there that may reveal clues that would only be visible to the eyes of a Keeper."

I sighed. "*Another* library? Just once, I'd like to search for clues in a mall or a coffeehouse."

Simon smiled. "The Vatican Library is a place like no other. Among other things, it houses the largest collection of occult-related literature in the world. You'll understand when you see it. Besides, it may be that someone there can explain how it is that Peraud and I look so much alike."

"A trick," I muttered. "Some dark magic."

"Maybe," Simon admitted. "But it's better to proceed with knowledge than guesses. And, since we've got a little extra time before we're due to meet Armand, I want to pursue something else here as well."

"Something else? Don't we *need* to find the next Board?"

"Of course we do," Simon said. "But getting you some help is more important at this point. If you're struggling with the strain of two Boards, adding another is only going to make things worse."

He had a point, but I hated admitting to weakness. "I'll be fine," I said. "I just need to get more rest."

"Maybe." Simon sounded skeptical. "But we'll explore it nonetheless. The Board will just have to wait a bit longer."

I was stunned at this, given how hard Simon had pushed us to get the Board of the Waters, and I was sure the two Boards I already had wouldn't like the idea, but getting any kind of assistance in dealing with them sounded too good to pass up. "Okay," I said. "So what's this idea?"

"There's a man here in Pompeii," Simon said. "Armand and I think he may be able to help you. His name is Dario Fidelis, and he is quite familiar with the Boards."

"How's that?" I asked. "It's not like these things come with instruction manuals."

"Più cappuccino, per favore. E gradiremmo i rulli pure," Simon said to the server who paused at our table. He nodded and came back with two more cappuccinos and a basket of rolls.

When he left, Simon continued. "No, they don't, and I don't suppose the Chronicle counts either. As it turns out, however, Dario knew your great-grandmother, Marissa Solitaire. At the time, he was a priest working for the Vatican in much the same capacity I do. Like I said, he's quite old, though Armand says he is still in remarkably good health."

"He *knew* her? That's amazing. How?" I asked.

Simon cleared his throat and looked away from me. "Apparently, they uh . . . lived together for a while. A long time ago."

I laughed. "That must have been quite the scandal in those days." The rolls were filled with apricot jelly of some kind, and I bit into one, closing my eyes in delight at the heavenly taste. "Don't mind me, I'm starved."

"I can see that," he said. "Anyway, this Dario lives here in Pompeii now—just down the road from the main entrance to the old ruins. Armand has let him know to expect us."

The Board of the Winds whispered in my mind. *"That is a name familiar to me, Keeper. The man he speaks of was your great-grandmother's first lover, before she came to America and took another for her husband."*

Even now, it was a disconcerting feeling to have a bodiless voice talking directly to my mind, though I'd gotten more used to it since I awakened the Board of the Waters. Simon was still unaware of how much the Boards knew and how often they spoke to me, and it didn't seem necessary to burden him with this knowledge. "How does Armand think this Dario can help?"

Simon shrugged. "He thinks it likely that Dario learned something about the Boards during his time with your great-grandmother. And he said that getting you some help seemed worth a shot, even from an unlikely source like this one."

Remembering how Saduj and Peraud had misled me in Israel, how easily I'd fallen for someone who was supposed to help me, I frowned. "As long as this guy is on the level, I'm willing to see him." I yawned again, and tried to hide it behind my mug. I paused, listening to the hissing language of the Boards conversing with each other, reminding me of why we were here. "Still, we can't spend too much time on it. We must find the Board of the Flames, and soon."

"If it means you getting some real sleep, I'm willing to take the time," Simon said. "We'll go see him as soon as we've finished our breakfast."

"Good," I said, finishing my roll and reaching for another one.

"Do you hear the cries of the dead, Keeper?" the Board of the Waters said. *"This place is filled with old spirits. Their cries for release echo from every pool of fresh water."*

"And in every breath of air," the Board of the Winds added.

I couldn't repress a shiver at the sudden change in topic. *"Why?"* I asked. *"What do they seek to be released from?"*

The Board of the Waters went silent, then said, *"Death is a very long time, Keeper."*

The Board of the Winds hissed, *"It is almost forever."*

I put the apricot roll back on my plate, my appetite gone. "If you don't mind, Simon, I'd like to see Dario sooner rather than later."

And the sooner I can find some way to silence these infernal Boards for a while, the better, I thought.

"My Lord, they have stopped their search for the next Board to meet with an elderly priest named Dario."

"He was a priest . . . but no longer. His love of the Keeper Marissa was his undoing, much as Simon will be undone by his true feelings for young Jenna. No doubt Dario's feelings for Marissa will be easily transferred to Jenna. Observe them, but do not reveal your presence—Jenna should be able to elicit some useful information from the old man. And in the end, that will only aid our true purposes."

I had expected Pompeii to be more like the outskirts of Naples, with little roads leading to small markets, and old men sitting on the sidewalks playing checkers. In reality, it was little more than a small village a couple of millennia old that had grown up across the road from the more ancient site. There were only two significant sources of income: tourism and vineyards. An ancient stone church near the entrance to the main archaeological site was still in service, holding what sounded like a morning Mass as Simon and I walked down the road together. Out of the corner of my eye, I saw Simon genuflect and mutter a brief prayer, but I pretended not to notice.

I had been raised Catholic, and had a healthy respect for the Church, but didn't practice regularly. I had almost as many unanswered questions about the Boards as I did about my faith, though I harbored no doubts about the power of God or the Boards. Simon's healing of Tom had proven that to me, if nothing else.

There were plenty of historic things to see, but the first thing I noticed was the stray dogs. Dozens of them, perhaps hundreds, roamed through the ruins and the surrounding streets. A good half dozen lounged near the Marina Gate—the harbor entry where ancient trade ships had sheltered—as we walked by. When they saw us, they let out of chorus of loud barks and howls and whimpers that sounded for all the world like they were trying to communicate with us.

"What do you make of that?" I asked Simon.

He shook his head. "I've been here many times, but I don't think I've ever seen the strays of Pompeii act like this before."

The Board of the Waters responded, *"They are the*

souls of the dead, Keeper, forced to remain here forever by the magic that destroyed their city long ago."

The Board of the Winds added, *"Or perhaps they merely sing to welcome you, Keeper of the Boards."*

I decided not to share these insights with Simon, and we continued past the gate and down into the more modern village proper, walking in silence and keeping our thoughts to ourselves. We'd been doing a lot of that since our trip to the Middle East, when Simon had kissed me to free me from the magical illusion cast by the incubus Saduj. But afterward, he had acted like nothing had happened between us.

But it *had* happened, and it had taken but one kiss for me to realize that despite the fact that he could be overprotective and arrogant, kissing him had felt so perfect, so *right*, that to not pursue what I felt for him seemed equally wrong. For now, I wanted more than he was willing to give, and it had made our partnership an uneasy one at times.

While I had dated off and on throughout high school and my first year of college, I'd never found anyone who seemed to fit with me the way Simon did. I had come to believe that we were meant to be together, just as much, if not more, than Simon believed I was meant to be the last Keeper of the Boards. More than ever, I was certain that many of the events in my life—including meeting Simon—were *supposed* to happen. . . . As the so-called

Daughter of Destiny, there seemed to be a lot about my life that wasn't in my control.

Typical, I thought. *I finally find a man that's not a demon,* and *that I'm truly interested in . . . and he's a committed priest. Perfect.*

"He matters not, Keeper. He fears your abilities. Your focus should be mastering your growing powers and on finding the other Boards. There will be time for more mundane pleasures later." The Board of the Waters, trying to be helpful with my love life. That was *just* what I needed right now.

I heard a scrabbling noise behind us, and turned to see nearly a dozen dogs loping after us a few yards away. When I stopped to look, they stopped as well, and once again chorused a cacophony of barks and howls. One in particular, a mongrel German shepherd with a matted tan-and-black coat and one blazing, golden eye, was especially loud and mournful.

I tugged on Simon's arm to get him to stop walking. "Do you suppose they're . . . ummm . . . trying to tell us something?" I asked.

He glanced behind us. "Not unless the message is 'feed me.'" He started walking again. "Come on, Jenna," he said. "Not everything is a force of magic. Let's just get to Dario's. They'll move on in a bit."

But they didn't. They followed us all the way to the

old stone house where we'd been told to find the ancient priest.

Simon rapped briskly on the door, doing his best to ignore the dogs and the stares of passersby.

From the other side, a voice cracked with age and marked by an Italian accent asked, "Who calls?"

"Simon Monk," he said. "And Jenna Solitaire."

"Come in, come in," the voice said. "The door is open."

Simon opened the door and stepped inside. I followed close behind and shut the door behind us. The interior of the house was dim, and a living area opened up to our immediate right. Several cushioned chairs and a small sofa filled the space.

In one chair, situated in a corner, was a man who looked so old that the first image that crossed my mind was of a living mummy. Yet as we drew closer, I saw that his shock of white hair was still vibrant, his skin wrinkled and liver spotted, but still supple. He stood as we neared, and I was immediately captured by his eyes. They were a brilliant shade of sky blue, bright enough they appeared nearly lit from within, and sparkling with intelligence.

He thrust a hand in my direction, which I accepted, and he shook firmly. "So, you're the new Keeper, are you? Jenna Solitaire?"

I nodded. "Yes," I said. "I'm Jenna Solitaire . . . the Keeper of the Boards."

"Hah!" the old man said, a wide smile on his face. "You even sound like her!" He held out both hands toward me, palms out. "May I?"

Unsure of what he wanted, I looked at Simon, who nodded. I didn't answer, and Dario moved closer, apparently taking my silence for consent. He very gently wrapped me in his arms in a tender hug. "Yes," he muttered, stepping back and wiping at his eyes. "You are the very image of your great-grandmother, Marissa. I never thought to see her like again, and yet here you are." He pointed to a large set of framed photographs on the wall. "There," he said. "Second from the left."

I slowly walked toward the images and saw an old black-and-white image of a woman dressed in a long, white gown. Tall and slender, with flowing hair that hung to her waist, she could have been my identical twin—the differences between us would have been almost unnoticeable.

"You see?" the old man whispered. "You can't tell from the picture, but even your hair color was the same. You look just like her."

"Yes," I said, stunned that I had never seen a picture of this woman, even among all of my grandmother's photo albums—and she had had plenty.

"And I am Dario," he said, shaking hands with Simon. "And you are Simon Monk, and now we're all properly introduced, rather than just pieces on a game board to that stuffed shirt, Armand."

Simon and I both laughed, knowing all too well how Armand loved his impeccable attire.

Dario cocked his head, listening, then said, "The dogs followed you here, didn't they, Jenna?"

"Yes, they did," I said. "It was the strangest thing."

"Barking and howling and generally making a nuisance of themselves, yes?" Dario pressed.

He may have been old, but he practically glowed with enthusiasm and energy. "Simon thought maybe they were looking for food," I said. "But I don't think so."

"No?" the old priest asked. "What do you think they were looking for?"

"Me," I said. "I think they were looking for me."

Dario laughed in delight and clapped his hands together. "Exactly right!" he said. "They've been looking for you for almost two thousand years." He grinned with obvious pleasure.

"Why?" Simon asked.

"Because it was a Keeper—Shalizander's daughter, in fact—who brought the Board of the Flames here, and it was the Board's magic that caused Vesuvius to erupt. And the magic that literally fell from the sky in the form of ash has trapped their souls here for all eternity—or until the magic of the Board is taken from Vesuvius."

"As dogs?" I asked.

"As *stray* dogs," Dario corrected. "They are souls without a home." He stared at me appraisingly, then turned to Simon. "How bad have things gotten for her?" he asked. "Is she sleeping at all?"

"Hey, don't talk about me like I'm not even here!" I protested.

"Asking you would be pointless," Dario said. "You'd only lie to make Simon or me feel better."

A little surprised by his insight, I didn't reply, and he spoke into the sudden silence, adding, "Jenna, the life of the Keeper is very . . . solitary, I think. Your family name suits that nature of the task you face. You confront challenges every day that would drive most people to the brink of insanity and beyond. Talking about them is important because it brings those demons into the light, just a little bit, where others can help you."

"But why should I burden you or Simon with problems only I can solve?" I asked.

"Only *you?* My Marissa felt much the same way," he said. "But it wasn't until she started talking to me, really talking, that the problems of dealing with her Board became manageable." He looked at me seriously. "The Boards want you disturbed. They want you weak, because it makes it easier for them to control you."

"Control me? But I thought—"

Sighing, Simon interrupted. "Personally, I think she's hanging by a thread. She doesn't sleep, can't eat anything more than fruit or bread, and the dreams are . . . terrible. When she does sleep, she usually wakes up screaming. She insists on reading that Chronicle, even though it makes her very sick every time she does."

"And the voices?" Dario asked, nodding and turning his attention back to me. "Just how much are the Boards talking to you, young Jenna Solitaire?"

"Do not listen to his lies, Jenna," the Board of the Waters said. *"Only we know how to unlock the power within you—how to help you open the way. All others only seek to control you for their own ends."*

Surprised at his knowledge, I felt myself pale and whispered, "All the time. They talk to me all the time and it's *never* quiet in my mind."

Eyes widening, Simon said, *"What?"* as his fingers released their hold on the coin necklace he touched when he was thinking or nervous.

Without a word, Dario stepped over to me and took me into his arms, holding me tight, like my grandfather had done when I was a frightened child. "I can help you, Jenna, and I will—if for no other reason than I once loved a Keeper . . . and I believe she once loved me."

"How?" I asked, tears filling my eyes. "How can you make it stop?"

"Shhh," he said, stroking my hair. He guided me to the couch and sat down with me. Taking my hands in his, he said, "I can't make it stop, Jenna. Only you can do that."

"But how?" Simon asked, still standing where he'd planted himself when we first entered the room.

"That," Dario said, "is precisely what I can teach her."

"How do you know all this? Who taught you?" I asked.

"Why, your great-great grandmother and I . . . we learned together, you might say." A mischievous smile softened his features. "We learned a great many different things, too."

Simon cleared his throat meaningfully. "I'm certain you did, but perhaps we should stay focused on the matters at hand?"

Dario shook his head at Simon's impertinence, like an adult silently admonishing an errant child. "We were both much younger then, which meant, of course, that we were willing to delve into mysteries often better left unexplored," Dario said. "And she only held one Board—the Board of the Winds, your birthright, Jenna—but she dreamed of the others, and we had planned to go together to find them."

"What happened?" I asked. "Why didn't you?"

His smile faded, and Dario looked at me in surprise. "You truly don't know, do you?" he asked.

"No," I said. "Know what?"

"She fled Italy, taking the Board with her, and went into hiding in America. She left me and demanded I stay far away from her forever."

"Why?" I asked. "Didn't she love you?"

"Yes," he said. "I believe she did—very much. Enough to do what she did and not question the price to her heart."

"Then why did she leave?" Jenna asked.

"Because an evil sorcerer wanted her Board—and all the others—for himself. And he was willing to hurt or even kill anyone to get his way." He gestured vaguely at his eyes. "To protect me, she left . . . and to protect myself, I gave up the priesthood, choosing to remain here instead."

"I'm . . . I'm sorry," I said. "I don't really know what else to say except that it's horrible."

"And it was," Dario said. "But I don't regret her decision or mine. I couldn't tell him where she had gone, because I didn't know then. I only learned later that she'd gone to America, and later still, that she had married your great-grandfather and produced a child."

"Why didn't this sorcerer just kill you?" Simon asked as he wrote quick notes in a small, leather-bound notebook that he'd produced from inside his jacket. He knew the ruthless nature of our enemies all too well.

"I only spoke to him once, after she left. He said it

would be more fitting to let me live alone, never to see or touch her again, than to kill me. Mercy, he told me, was not a quality he was very familiar with." Dario laughed grimly. "It appears, however, that he misjudged the future, for on this day I am no longer alone—I can see and hear her as though she were still alive."

"What happened to this sorcerer? What was his name?" Simon asked.

"I do not know," Dario said. "Perhaps he lives still— and if he does, then he is still seeking the Boards—and you, young Jenna."

"It makes sense that Peraud isn't working alone," Simon said, his mouth a grim line. "Armand mentioned that his magical skills have grown exponentially in the last few years. Perhaps this ancient sorcerer, whoever he is, is training him somehow."

"One problem at a time," I said, forcibly dismissing the idea that there was a stronger power behind Peraud. "I'll deal with ancient sorcerers hunting me later. First, can you tell me how to get to the Board of the Flames? My . . . visions have told me that it's here, in Mount Vesuvius, but I don't know how to get there."

"Jenna," Simon said. "Let's just hold off a bit. We've got some time. Let Dario help you if he can."

"Your friend is right," Dario said firmly. "Getting the Board of Flames . . . I know you are driven to seek it out, but before we do that, we must first do something else."

"What would that be?" I asked. "If we go get the Board now, before Peraud gets here, then we can take all the time we need with Dario, because we'll already have it."

"Already, the Boards, rather than your common sense, are dictating your actions," Dario said. "How will you be able to handle a third Board, young Jenna, when the first two have already pushed you to your limits?"

I sighed, knowing that he was right, but hating the delay all the same. "All right," I agreed. "What must we do first?"

"You must learn to listen," the old priest said. "So that you may learn the language of control and power, the Language of the Birds." He patted me on the hand. "And control is what you need more than anything—over your mind first, and then over the Boards. The Language of the Birds—that is, the language spoken by man before the fall of the Tower of Babel, when all of mankind spoke only one tongue—is the key to that control."

"If it means getting to the Board of the Flames, *and* being able to sleep without dreaming for once, I'd learn Sanskrit," I said.

Outside, the dogs began howling again, and I added, "Or even how to talk dog."

"Well, I don't think *that* will be necessary anyway,"

he said. "Which is good, because I don't speak dog all that well." He chuckled at his own joke, then gestured at my pack. "Shall we get started?"

I nodded and took the Boards out of my backpack and set them on the table. Each Board was roughly triangular in shape, with an odd arc cut from one side that descended down like a crescent moon.

Dario put his hands out over them, then nodded to himself. "Why do you have them separated?" he asked.

"What do you mean? Each Board is individual," I said.

Dario shook his head. "Not at all," he said. "The Boards were designed to work individually, but only together do they achieve their greatest powers. They fit together like a puzzle."

"How did you know that?"

"I'm observant," he said. "Look closely at the edges. Do you see those tiny slots? The only purpose they could serve is to attach to something else."

I picked up the Board of the Winds and held it up so I could see the edge. Sure enough, very small slots patterned the edge of the Board. "Amazing," I said.

"Now," he said, "take the other Board and slide them together. You should feel a faint . . . locking sensation when you do."

I put the Board of the Winds down on the table and slid the Board of the Waters next to it. It was almost at though they melded together, because suddenly they were one solid unit. "Why didn't I think of that?" I muttered, looking at the new shape they made when combined. "It doesn't make them any less unwieldy, but you can't have everything, I suppose."

"Ahhh," Dario said. "Using them both at the same time should be a bit easier for you now, but to answer how to make them less inconvenient to carry around, I'm afraid I don't know. In looking at them, though, I don't think that's the only way they can be assembled."

"How so?" Simon asked from his chair across the room.

Dario shrugged. "Nothing about the Boards is simple, young man, and little is as it appears. Were I to guess, I would say that when you have all the Boards of a set together, their shape may be completely different, creating some kind of 'Master' Board, if you will."

"A Master Board," Simon said, his voice quiet and curious. "I suppose that does make a certain amount of sense, especially when you consider that the first group of Boards is sometimes called the Boards of the Elements, while other Boards are referred to by different group names. But how do you imagine they change their shape?"

Impatient to get on with the lessons, I interrupted and said, "Gentlemen, perhaps we can talk Board theory some other time. For right now, I just want to get a good night's sleep."

Dario laughed, and even Simon smiled.

"Very well," Dario said. "We can discuss that later."

Simon looked miffed—he loved learning new things, exploring esoteric possibilities—but he nodded. "Okay, but it's worth coming back to at some point. It may be useful information later on."

"More like speculation," I said. "But we can talk more about it later."

"Good," Dario said. "The first word you must learn is this: *Vixisthra*." When I didn't say anything, he said, "Go ahead, try it."

The word sounded strangely familiar, and the tone was very much like the voices of the Boards. "What does it mean?" I asked.

The Board of the Waters's voice sounded like water rushing over rocks, a tone from it that I had come to associate with annoyance. *"It is a command word in the old tongue, Keeper,"* it said. *"It means 'silence.'"*

The Board of the Winds chimed in, adding, *"It will . . . compel us to remain quiet for a time, but our counsel is more important than silence."*

"*Vixisthra!*" I said. The Boards immediately fell silent. I grinned, exulting in the sudden peace and quiet in my mind. "Oh, I like this word very much already."

"Excellent," Dario said, sharing my smile. "A bit more emphasis on the 'r,' and you'll have it completely."

I repeated the word several times until Dario was satisfied and I had committed it to memory. The Boards had not whispered again since I first spoke the word. "How long will it keep them quiet?" I asked him.

"A short time," Dario said. "Perhaps an hour or two. A bit longer if they choose to be cooperative with your desire for silence."

Simon, sitting on a chair across the room, said, "What if she wants them to start talking to her again?"

"Then she should say *grametex*," Dario said. "It means 'speak.'"

"*Grametex!*" I said. I expected to hear the Boards' voices clamor in my mind, yet they remained silent, as if proving that they did not have to speak all the time. *Fine, be that way*, I thought, and returned my attention to Dario.

"Those are words of command and power, Jenna," Dario said. "From what you call the Language of the Birds, though they have not been uttered in many years. Not since your great-grandmother lived."

The Board of the Winds spoke, its voice an eerie, echoing tone—stronger and more insistent than I had ever heard it sound. "*She sought to master me, Keeper. And her ignorant use of the old tongue drew the attention of many supernatural creatures.*"

"The Board of the wind is saying that my great-grandmother Marissa drew the attention of supernatural creatures when she tried to master them using words like these."

JENNA SOLITAIRE

Dario smiled grimly. "It said the exact same thing to her about someone who had possessed the Board earlier. The Boards are not above *lying*, Jenna. You must remember that."

"What *are* the Boards exactly?" Simon asked. "In all my research, I haven't been able to find a real answer."

"Alas, you won't find one here, either," Dario said. "At least not a certain one. Most of what I know comes from guessing and the hints that Marissa and I were able to get from her Board. We were convinced that the Boards are some kind of conscious, supernatural entities trapped within the magical framework of each individual artifact. Perhaps they are elementals of some kind."

"I don't think so," I said, shuddering. "The Board of the Flames can summon fire elementals, so that doesn't seem quite right."

"It can?" Simon asked, jotting more notes. "Was that what you dreamed about last night?"

I nodded. "Yes. There was a Keeper who had three of the Boards—Air, Water, and Fire—and they . . . ." My voice trailed off as I remembered the dream.

"She also tried to master us, Keeper," the Board of the Waters said.

"And paid the price for her ignorance and arrogance," the Board of the Winds added.

"They what?" Simon asked.

"Betrayed her," I said. "They waited until she'd summoned three massive fire elementals, and then they . . . they left her, and wouldn't respond to her commands."

"I have never heard of such a thing," Simon said. "The Keeper of the Boards is . . . I don't know, the person who is supposed to use them, to be in control of them."

"Nor have I," Dario admitted. "Perhaps it was just a dream, and not a truth."

I shook my head. "It was both a dream and the truth. They betrayed her, and left her to die."

"We work with the Keeper willingly, but we are not her slaves, subject to her every whim," the Board of the Waters said. *"She violated this and paid the price."*

"She was warned," the Board of the Winds said.

"How did she violate this?" I asked.

"She would not seek out the Board of the Earth, nor the key to becoming the Master of the Elements."

"She would not open the way."

"What does that mean?" I asked. *"To open the way."*

"This is a truth which shall be revealed to you in time," the Board of the Waters replied.

"When you are ready," the Board of the Winds said.

I sighed. "The Boards . . . ." I started to tell Simon and Dario what the Boards had said, but decided it didn't matter. There wasn't anything in their words worth sharing except vague warnings about some Keeper long since dead. "Never mind," I finished. "Let's just keep going."

"I think," Simon said, "that we'll know more once we have all four Boards. For now, all we can do is speculate that they will gain in power, giving you abilities relating to all the prime elements."

"I don't even have power over my own life," I said. "Let alone any of the elements. I'm just beginning to really learn how to use the Boards. Dario, have you ever heard of any of that?"

"Yes," he said. "Long ago, when your great-grandmother still held the Board of the Winds. It spoke to her about the opening of the way, though it refused to explain what that meant, other than continually insisting that she seek out the other Boards."

"Just once, I'd like to have complete information to go on," I said.

"Wouldn't we all?" asked Simon. "Perhaps part of the role of Keeper is to discover information about the Boards, rather than just having the power handed to her."

"You have the Chronicle, don't you?" Dario asked. "There is much you can learn from those pages—the history of the Boards and the Keepers who held them is contained therein."

"It makes her ill and disoriented to read it," Simon said. "I've discouraged her."

Dario sighed. "An unfortunate effect of the magic of the Chronicle," he said. "But it is the most complete source of information on the Boards that I know of."

"Is there any way around it?" I asked. "I've read parts of the Chronicle, but what I'd love to do is read it from cover to cover."

"You can't," Dario said. "The Chronicle's magic prevents you from doing so. Marissa and I discovered that early on, soon after she had first obtained the Board of the Winds." He fell silent for a minute, lost in memory. "Haven't you noticed," he asked, "how whenever you open the Chronicle looking for something—say, information on the Board of the Waters—you always find a place that refers to your question right away?"

"Yes," I said. "But I just assumed—"

"So did we," he said. "At first, anyway. But if you tried to read it from cover to cover, just reading it, you'd become terribly ill. Marissa tried and spent about three days barely conscious."

"But why?" Simon asked. "Why would Shalizander have made it that way?"

"Who knows?" Dario replied. "The only conclusion I ever came to about it was that it was an additional protection—to keep the Keepers from learning too much too quickly or from attempting things they weren't ready to handle."

The Board of the Waters laughed in my mind, a gurgling brook sound that was disturbing. *Shalizander had no such noble intentions,* it said. *Her goal was to ensure that future Keepers never matched her own powers.*

"If she was going to be dead by then, why bother?" I asked.

"If she was going to be dead . . . ." the Board replied.

"What do you mean 'if?" I asked.

"What makes you believe that one of Shalizander's magical prowess would not have found a way to cheat death itself?"

The very idea seemed . . . wrong to me. Everyone died, didn't they? *"Did she?"* I demanded. *"Did Shalizander find a way to cheat death?"*

For a long time, both Boards remained silent. Then the watery voice of the Board of the Waters filled my mind. *"Her physical body died, but the body is only a shell. What happened to her spirit . . . that is knowledge we do not . . . possess."*

I shivered, thinking of what that ability would truly mean in the wrong hands. An evil wizard like Peraud would use magic such as that to wreak havoc for centuries; a wriggling, malignant worm in the apple of time itself.

I wondered what Simon would think of the idea, but dismissed the notion of asking him. I had no doubt, being raised Catholic myself, that he would consider the idea both absurd and disturbing.

Personally, I found it terrifying.

"Hear me, Peraud."

"Yes, my Lord?"

"Things are moving too slowly to suit me. It is time to speed our timetable up a bit. Contact Simon. Arrange that matter we spoke of earlier, make sure it happens away from town. He is distracting her, and I do not want anything to get in the way of the Keeper's training."

"It shall be done, my Lord."

"Contact me as soon as you are finished. I have an idea that will work to our advantage, and enable us to accomplish more than we ever have before."

"I think," Dario said as we fell silent, "that we've wandered a bit far afield. There is more I can teach you, but not today. We will resume tomorrow."

"That's a good idea," Simon said. "I'm ready to stretch my legs anyway." He stood and shrugged into his long, black, light canvas trench coat that made him look even taller than he was. It also complemented the black clothing and white collar of a priest.

"Thank you, Dario," I said. I gathered up the Boards, now a solid unit, and struggled for a moment to fit the awkward shape into the opening of my backpack. I finally managed to get them put away, but pretty soon, I'd have to find a better way to carry them around.

"You are most welcome, young Jenna," he said, his wrinkled face lighting up with a smile. "I know you seek the Board of the Flames, and I have no doubt that it's here . . . deep inside Vesuvius itself, as your visions have shown. We will find a path that leads you to it, but in due time, when you're ready for the added burden."

He reached out and took my hands, then kissed one of them lightly. "I would help you anyway," he said, "but for Marissa's sake, I will help you even more."

"You're very sweet," I told him. Simon handed me my jean jacket, which I put on, then we walked to the door. I had expected early spring in southern Italy to be warmer, but for the most part, I'd been stuck with a jacket and a turtleneck since we'd arrived.

"You have our thanks," Simon said. "Have a good evening."

"Just watch after her, young man," Dario said. "That will be thanks enough."

We stepped out into the late-afternoon sunlight, and I blinked several times. The cool air felt good on my face after being inside for so long. The dogs were still there, gathered in a small pack around the golden-eyed German shepherd I'd seen earlier. The minute I stepped outside they began barking and howling.

"Wonderful," Simon said. "Are they going to do this the entire time we're here?"

"Apparently," I said. "Shoo! Go on!" I waved my arms at the dogs, but they refused to leave.

From the doorway behind us, Dario cleared his throat. "Say the word *bilaxt* to them," he said. "It means 'begone.'"

"They speak the Language of the Birds?" Simon asked. "They're *dogs*."

"Correction," Dario said. "They are very old spirits trapped in the form of dogs. Go ahead, Jenna, try it."

"Bilaxt!" I said.

Several of the dogs yelped, and most of them took off across the street, running into the nearby ruins. All of them except the German shepherd. "Well, it worked," I said. "For the most part."

"That one doesn't seem to want to leave," Simon said.

"I noticed," I muttered. I knelt down and whistled softly. "Come here, girl," I said. "Come on."

The dog whined quietly, then wagged her tail and

came forward. She sniffed at my upraised palms and my clothes, then sneezed twice and sat down next to me.

"You have a new friend," Dario said from behind me. "We can always use new friends."

"That's for sure," I said. I turned my attention to Simon. "I guess we're stuck with this one, but it beats having the whole pack of them follow us around. It would be embarrassing to show up at the hotel with every stray dog in Pompeii in tow."

Simon heaved a weary sigh and then thanked Dario once more before starting off down the street. I followed a step or two behind, and the dog kept pace with me. "I wonder what her name is?" I asked Simon's back.

"Dog," he suggested sourly. His tone of voice suggested he wasn't very happy with our newfound companion.

"Her name is *not* Dog," I said. "And what's your problem, anyway?"

"Nothing," he said. "At least nothing more than usual."

"Simon, stop right there," I said.

He turned and stared at me. "What?"

"What *is* your problem?" I asked. "We stepped outside and suddenly you're in a foul mood."

"You don't get it, do you, Jenna?" he asked. "These dogs—that dog—aren't normal! We don't need to be any more visible than we already are, and now we've added a one-eyed German shepherd that understands a dead language to our traveling show. This isn't a family vacation, you know. We have to move light and fast to get the Boards before Peraud does, and having an animal to take care of will only slow us down."

"Hold on a minute!" I said. "I didn't say I was adopting the dog, or anything of the sort. It's not like I have a choice in where stray dogs hang out."

"You should send her away," Simon said. "The spirits of the dead . . . ." His voice trailed off, and he sighed. "I'm sorry, Jenna. There are some things that truly disturb my sense of . . . order in the universe. The spirits of once-living humans being trapped and kept from the next world is one of them. Possession in any form is *evil*."

There was a lovely thought to cap my day, and I shook my head. "I understand what you're saying," I said. "But it's not like I went to a local kennel and picked her out. She picked me." As soon as the words left my mouth I knew they were right. She *had* picked me. For some reason.

Simon leaned closer to me, holding me by the shoulders. "And *that* doesn't concern you, Jenna? That she somehow *picked* you?" He sighed, shaking his head, and I felt his hands tighten on my arms. "I hate to see you taking unnecessary risks."

"It's not an unnecessary risk," I said, enjoying the rare closeness between us. He rarely touched me, and I thought the time had come to address another issue. "Beside, I don't think the dog is what has you so upset."

"Then what has me so upset?" Simon said, his gaze locked with mine.

"Us," I said. "What we feel."

"Jenna," he said, pulling away so suddenly I almost fell. "I think we've already talked about this."

"What are you so afraid of, Simon? That you might like it? That you might *feel* something for someone else? What if we're *supposed* to be together, Simon? Have you ever thought about that? That the kiss we shared in Petra . . . us, our relationship . . . that it's supposed to happen. Just like you say I was supposed to be the 'Daughter of Destiny.' On top of everything else, we shouldn't have to be alone, too."

"Jenna, we've been through this," he said. "I am a priest, and whether I'm interested in a deeper relationship with you or not is immaterial. It is forbidden." He turned and started walking back down the street.

"Then why did you touch me that way just now? I can feel, you know. You're sending mixed signals!"

Without turning around, Simon said, "Let's just get back to the hotel and find some dinner. I'll arrange to have the dog stay in your room."

Trying not to respond to his words about a deeper relationship between us being immaterial, trying to keep the hurt from my face, was hard. I felt my jaw muscles clench and searched from something to say, finally coming up with a muttered, "That'll cost extra." Knowing how much he hated spending money he thought was unnecessary, he was sure to complain about it, and maybe it would distract him from how he'd just hurt me.

"With you, it seems everything does," he said.

We walked the rest of the way back to the hotel in silence, and if it weren't for the dog's company, it would have felt like I was walking the evening streets of Pompeii all alone.

After dinner that night, I checked my BlackBerry for a connection and found that I could go online without any serious problems. Right away, I saw that Kristen was online and I sent her an instant message.

BQUEEN: HEY YOU!
  SMLTWNWITCH: JENNA! WHERE ARE YOU? ARE YOU OKAY?
  BQUEEN: I'M FINE. I'M SICK OF LIVING IN HOTEL ROOMS. SIMON AND I ARE IN POMPEII NOW, LOOKING FOR THE NEXT BOARD.

SMLTWNWITCH: THAT'S WHAT TOM TOLD ME. ARE YOU EVER GOING TO GET A BREAK? ALL YOU'VE DONE IS RUN, RUN AND RUN SOME MORE. CAN'T YOU TAKE SOME TIME OFF?

BQUEEN: NOT YET. SOME DAYS IT SEEMS LIKE ALL I'LL EVER GET TO DO AGAIN IS TRY TO FIND THE NEXT BOARD, AND THE ONE AFTER THAT, AND SO ON. THE GOOD NEWS IS THAT I FINALLY FOUND SOME REAL HELP.

SMLTWNWITCH: <GROAN> NOT ANOTHER NEW MAN IN YOUR LIFE?!

BQUEEN: LOL! NO, NOT EXACTLY. HIS NAME IS DARIO AND HE WAS A PRIEST, BUT GET THIS—HE KNEW MY GREAT-GRANDMOTHER MA-RISSA. THEY WERE LOVERS!

SMLTWNWITCH: WOW! YOU'RE KIDDING. HOW *OLD* IS THIS GUY?

BQUEEN:I DON'T KNOW, BUT OLD ENOUGH TO HAVE KNOWN HER. THE GOOD NEWS IS THAT HE KNOWS A LOT ABOUT THE BOARDS AND IS HELPING ME LEARN TO CONTROL THEM. MY FIRST GOAL IS A GOOD NIGHT'S SLEEP. ONCE THAT'S ACCOMPLISHED, CONQUERING THE UNI-VERSE SHOULD BE A SNAP!

SMLTWNWITCH: AT LEAST YOU STILL HAVE YOUR SENSE OF HUMOR. HOW ARE YOU AND SI-MON GETTING ALONG?

BQUEEN: <SIGH> WE'RE OKAY, I GUESS. HE'S STARTED WEARING THE WHITE COLLAR AND BLACK SUIT AGAIN. IT ONLY MAKES HIM LOOK MORE ATTRACTIVE. BETWEEN THE CLOTHING AND THE ACCENT, HE LOOKS LIKE HE SHOULD BE IN AN ARTY EUROPEAN MOVIE.

SMLTWNWITCH: HE'LL COME AROUND IN TIME. YOU ARE IRRESISTIBLE, YOU KNOW.

BQUEEN: AND YOU ARE SWEET. HOW ARE YOU FEELING?

SMLTWNWITCH: I'M GOOD, J., I REALLY AM. AND TOM IS GETTING BETTER EVERY DAY. EVERYTHING THAT REALLY COUNTS STILL WORKS, AND THAT'S WHAT'S IMPORTANT.

BQUEEN: 'EVERYTHING'? <VBG> I'M TEASING YOU, OF COURSE. WHAT ARE YOU GOING TO DO ONCE TOM IS FULLY MENDED?

SMLTWNWITCH: I'M GOING TO FIND THAT PERAUD CHARACTER AND KICK HIS BUTT.

BQUEEN: LOL! WELL, WHAT SAY YOU LET ME HANDLE THE EVIL WIZARDS FOR NOW AND YOU JUST CONCENTRATE ON HELPING TOM GET BETTER?

SMLTWNWITCH: OKAY, BUT AT THE LEAST, I'M COMING TO GET YOU AND BRING YOU HOME FOR A LONG REST.

BQUEEN: I'VE GOT TO GO, BUT I LOVE YOU

BOTH AND I'LL WRITE AGAIN SOON. I
PROMISE.

SMLTWNWITCH: WAIT! TOM JUST CAME IN AND
WANTS TO KNOW IF WE CAN DO ANYTHING TO
HELP YOU.

BQUEEN: HMMM . . . I DON'T KNOW. THERE
IS ONE THING, BUT IT'S NOT DIRECTLY RE-
LATED TO THE BOARDS.

SMLTWNWITCH: NAME IT.

BQUEEN: I WANT TO KNOW MORE ABOUT
MY FAMILY. FOR EXAMPLE, MY GREAT-
GRANDMOTHER MARISSA, WHO WAS THE FIRST
OF OUR FAMILY TO COME TO AMERICA.

SMLTWNWITCH: GENEALOGY RESEARCH, HUH?
WELL, IT'S NOT MAGIC AND HIGH ADVENTURE,
BUT WE'LL DO WHAT WE CAN. WHY THE INTER-
EST?

BQUEEN: A HUNCH. THE MORE I KNOW ABOUT
MY FAMILY, THE MORE—MAYBE—I CAN UNDER-
STAND ABOUT THE BOARDS. TALK TO YOU GUYS
SOON, OKAY? LOVE YA!

SMLTWNWITCH: LOVE YOU, TOO.

After signing off, I put the BlackBerry away and shut
off the light. The moon shone in through my window,
and I mentally probed the Boards' presence.

"Are you going to let me sleep tonight?"

"We do not disturb your rest without purpose, Keeper," the Board of the Winds said. *"Your dreams are dreams of power, dreams of dominion, dreams of past Keepers and their eventual failures. These are all necessary lessons, to ensure your ability to do what must be done to open the way."*

"Why? All they do is exhaust and frighten me."

"They are only dreams, Keeper, and you have always had vivid dreams," the Board of the Waters said. *"But these dreams are not the affliction you must focus on. The Chronicle is the true source of the dreams."*

"The Chronicle? How? Why?"

"We do not know," they said. *"Perhaps it is how Shalizander meant things to be for all her descendants."*

"What do you mean?"

"Perhaps she desired them to be . . . ."

"To be?"

"Needful of her assistance."

"But she's dead!"

"Of course . . . ."

On the floor, the dog whined in her sleep. I shushed her, thinking that I'd have to come up with a name of some kind. "Dog" was out of the question. Feeling my eyelids grow heavy, I let them close, and wondered what dreams would come that night. What the Boards meant with their strange talk of the Chronicle and Shalizander.

And if someday, seeing my death in those dreams would bring me death in the real world.

The voices are distant and familiar. In the dark void of my dream, I can hear them, but I see nothing. All is black and there is only the voice of the Wind, hissing and swirling, and the voice of the Water, gurgling and low. They speak the Language of the Birds, and they are planning . . . something. I know it.

Even as I sleep, they plot. If only I could understand what they are saying!

"We speak of many things, Keeper," the Board of the Winds says. "We speak of the future, of the past, of Keepers that have failed and those that have failed to try."

"Try what?" I ask.

"To open the way," it replies.

I know they will not answer the obvious question, so I choose another. "What is required to open the way?"

The Boards laugh, and the sounds are Earth sounds: a spring wind rushing across open fields, water rolling over a rocky streambed. "Very good, Keeper. You will come to understand the rules we are bound by in time," the Board of the Waters says.

"The first requirement of opening the way is possession

of the thirteen Boards of Babylon," the Board of the Winds intones. "No Keeper shall open the way without holding all of them."

Exulted by this information, I ask, "Do all thirteen Boards still exist?"

"Of course, Keeper. We cannot be destroyed by any mortal means," the Board of the Waters replies. There is a pause; then it adds, "There is a second requirement."

"The second requirement of opening the way is complete mastery of each of the Master Boards, of which there are three," the Board of the Winds says.

"What are the three Master Boards?" I ask, thrilling to this new knowledge.

"Is she ready?" the Board of the Winds asks.

"She asks," the Board of the Waters replies. "We are bound to respond to this line of questioning."

"We are also allowed judgment! To respond as we see fit."

"She is the last," the Board of the Waters says. "If she fails, all is lost and the way will never be opened!"

For several minutes, the two Boards argue, but in the Language of the Birds. I do not understand what they are saying, and my frustration grows. I speak several times, and when they refuse to hear me, I remember the words Dario taught me.

"Vixisthra!" I scream into the void.

The Boards fall immediately silent.

"I am the Keeper of the Boards," I say. "I will judge when I am ready and when I am not, for the burden has fallen to me. There is and will be no other." I wait for the echoes of my words to fade, then say, "Grametex."

As one, in the strangely powerful voice I heard earlier, the two Boards say, "Your will is my will, Keeper."

"What are the three Master Boards?" I ask.

"She learns quickly. The priest is teaching her the vocabulary of power."

"She will need it when the time comes. The opening of the way requires it. Answer her question, Brother, and then she must rest."

"Keeper, there are three Master Boards, each created from lesser Boards, such as myself and my brother. The first Master Board is the Board of the Elements. To hold it, one must possess the Board of the Winds, the Board of the Waters, the Board of the Flames, and the Board of the Earth. When properly combined and awakened, this Master Board will give you power over all the primary elements of the Earth."

The implications of this are myriad, but I press on. "And the other two?"

"The others . . . will be made known to you in due time."

"Tell me something!" I say.

"I will name the next set of Boards for you, Keeper,

that you may remember them when the time is right. The next set of Boards are referred to as the Boards of Lesser Lifeforms. Individually, they are known as the Board of the Swarms, the Board of the Wings, the Board of the Skins, and the Board of the Live Bearers."

What had these ancient sorcerers created? I wonder. "And the others? The last set?"

"She is treading on dangerous ground, Brother. We should wait. Remember the others!"

"She has asked. We must provide an answer."

"Not necessarily the answer she seeks!"

There was a long pause, and then, "Ask again at another time, Keeper. Ask after you have successfully obtained the first four Boards, and I shall provide you the answer you seek."

"Why will you not tell me now?" I ask.

"Because too much knowledge at the wrong time can be a dangerous thing, Keeper," the Board of the Winds says.

I feel like something is missing, some critical piece of information, but I am uncertain of what it might be. "And then, when I have them all, the way will be opened?" I ask.

"No, Keeper," the Board of the Waters says. "Then you will have the means to open the way, but not the key."

"What is the key?" I ask.

"We do not know," the Board replies. "It is said that

when you have all the Boards, the knowledge of the key will become apparent."

Desperate, I ask, "Do you have any idea at all?"

"This secret is lost to time itself, Keeper. It may be that this information is held by one of our brothers."

"Has any other Keeper attempted to open the way, to gather all of the Boards?"

The Board of the Winds replies. "Many times, Keeper."

"And?" I prompt.

"They failed, Keeper. No one has ever held more than the first two Boards of the Elements at one time, with the exception of Shalizander and her first daughter, Malizander."

"None were strong enough," the Board of the Waters adds. "You are."

"Why did they fail?" I ask.

"Death comes to all humans, Keeper," the Board of the Winds says. "We are not used lightly."

"So they tried and it killed them."

"We would say that they tried and circumstance killed them. They were weak. You are strong."

"You are the last," the Board of the Waters says. "You will succeed where the others failed."

"What if I quit? What if I don't want all those powers?"

The Boards laugh, and this time the sounds are of a

*dying Earth: of land ripped asunder and entire conti-
nents crumbling into the ocean. "You have no choice,
Keeper," the Board of the Winds whispers. "Once you
awakened me, the path was laid out before you. This is
why so many of your ancestors did not awaken me. You
cannot stop, except in death. If you try, the dreams will
torment you, night after night, until you are no longer
able to tell dream from reality. You will long for your life
to end, if only to stop the madness."*

"And you ache for the power," a new voice says.

*The Boards are silent, a sense of waiting and watch-
ing filling the void. A sense of fear.*

"Who is there?" I ask.

*"You have learned enough, I think, for one night. Per-
haps too much."*

"But I—"

"Awaken!" the unfamiliar voice commands.

*A wave of pain shoots through my body, and it hits
like a jolt of lightning. I resist the urge to scream.*

"Awaken!"

*Another jolt, and this time the void is lit up from some
distant place and I see that it is a void. Empty of everything except what I put there . . . or what finds me there.
Suddenly, I am afraid. Afraid of knowledge, of knowing
more. Afraid of the voice I do not know.*

Afraid of death.

"Awaken!" the voice commands for a third time.

A blue bolt of energy leaps across the grayness of the void and slams into me. I cannot resist the pain.

I scream, and the dream ends.

"My Lord, it has been done as you commanded."
"Excellent, Peraud. You have pleased me,
particularly in light of your previous efforts. Now go,
and resume your position in the town. I think there
will be need of you there . . . soon."

I opened my eyes to see the early-morning sunlight filtering in through the window, my throat raw with an unvoiced scream. And there was the German shepherd, staring expectantly at me.

"What?" I asked, thinking again that she needed a name. The dog whined softly and pushed her nose against my face. "Okay," I muttered. "I'll get up."

I threw back the covers and climbed out of bed. "Amber," I said to the dog, thinking of another set of amber eyes that had caught my attention in Jerusalem. I had fallen for a man named Saduj, whose eyes had been the color of honey in sunlight. Even when his true nature and appearance were revealed, his eyes had still been beautiful.

I did not consider what had happened between me and Saduj as something to be ashamed of, but as something to learn from—mainly, that I needed to be cautious and that the choices I made could profoundly affect others. "I think I'll call you Amber," I said to the dog. If nothing else, she could serve as a reminder of my past lesson.

The dog didn't reply, but walked to the door of the hotel room and scratched at it. "Want out?" I asked. "Just let me get dressed first, okay?"

With another soft whine, Amber circled a couple of times and then lay down in front of the door. For a stray, she was an incredibly well-behaved dog, even co-operating when I'd first put her in the bathtub the night before. Her cooperation was short-lived, however, because when I tried to scrub her down with shampoo, she'd resisted, twisting and turning in my arms, until finally I'd used all my strength, picked her up, and plopped her down in the bubble-filled bathtub. I apparently won the war of wills, though she looked up at me with bubbles caught in her fur and barked once, as if to say, "So? I don't *have* to be in here."

"Yes, you do," I'd said, then had proceeded to scrub her down as thoroughly as possible. After a few minutes, she'd gotten into it herself, arching her back and groaning in pleasure as I massaged shampoo into her coat. By the time we were done, I felt filthy and soaked, but the dog was clean, and between us, we'd managed to get through it with only four towels and a floor mat truly the worse for the wear.

I quickly dressed and pulled my long hair into a ponytail as I thought about the dream from the night before. It was then I realized something else—I felt fully rested and awake. For the first time in weeks, even before I had found the Board of the Winds. I wondered if the Boards had done something to help with that, but decided they probably hadn't. It wasn't in their nature to care about anything human. Most likely, it was learning some of the Language of the Birds and feeling like I was a little more in control.

The strange voice in the dream was disturbing, though. Had it been the voice of another Board, or something—*someone* maybe—darker still? Could it have been Peraud? I shook my head. Another mystery for me to solve, but at least this time, I wouldn't be alone. I could talk to Simon, but I could also talk to Dario. He was a sweet old man, and I was sure he would try to help with anything I needed.

I pulled on my beat-up denim jacket and grabbed my backpack. "All right, Amber, let's go," I said, opening the door. We went downstairs, and I saw that Simon was already up and having a cup of coffee and a hard roll in the outdoor café across the street. I stood for a moment and watched him as he read the morning paper, his chiseled features somewhat softer and careworn in the morning sun. He looked up, saw me, and smiled, and I felt my heart beat a little faster. Just a glance from him was enough to make me smile in return.

Traffic was almost nonexistent, and Amber and I crossed the street without difficulty. She sniffed his pant leg, then found a small grassy area to do her business before settling down on the sidewalk to stare at me. There was something unsettling about her direct gaze, and it wasn't just a sense of being watched—it was the sense that she was waiting for me to do something.

I sat down across from Simon and said, "Good morning."

"Good morning," he replied. "You seem chipper today. Did you get some sleep?"

Signaling for the waiter to bring another cup of coffee, I nodded. "Yes, I did. Sort of. Though it was strange. I had a very odd dream."

As the waiter prepared to pour my coffee, Simon shook his head, putting a hand out to cover my cup. "You don't want that," he said, pointing at the coffeepot in the server's hand. "Order an espresso or a cappuccino. The regular coffee is terrible."

"You know me so well," I said. I tried to ask the

server for a cappuccino, but my attempt at speaking Italian was a disaster, though the word "cappuccino" got through okay.

Simon took pity on me, and a faint smile softened his features. *"Porta alla signora un cappuccino, per favore,"* he said, and the server nodded and wandered back into the restaurant to make it.

"What was your dream about?" Simon asked, handing me a roll.

"I don't even know if it really was a dream," I said. I told him about the Boards and what they'd said, and he listened quietly while I spoke. I didn't tell him about the strange voice at the end, since it made little sense to me and I wanted to ask Dario about it first.

"That's incredible!" Simon said. "Knowing the names will be massively important in our search for the other Boards." He paused, looking thoughtful, then added, "And it's scary. The power of each set of Boards seems to escalate. I'm trying to imagine what the powers of the final set might be, and why the Boards were created that way."

"I'm pretty sure it will be something major," I said, "but for now, just getting the *next* Board is going to be challenge enough, I think."

"Agreed," he said. He took another sip from his mug, staring at Amber. "What do you make of her?"

The server brought my cappuccino, which I took

gratefully. "I don't know," I said, noticing how she cocked her head to one side as though she were listening to our conversation. "She's not a normal dog, that's certain."

"If what Dario says is true," Simon said, "then her soul is human in origin, trapped in the body of a dog."

"Fair enough," I said. "But the question I have is if there are thirteen Boards, and no one has ever managed to get more than the first three, where does that leave me?"

"You are different," Simon said. "As soon as you've finished working with Dario, we'll get the Board of the Flames and keep going on to the others. We'll get through it all together."

"Be assured, Keeper, you are the last," the Board of the Winds said.

"As foretold by Shalizander's prophecy," the Board of the Waters added.

Ignoring them both, I directed my questions at Simon. "But why? What is it about me that makes me the one?"

"Shalizander's line ends with you," Simon said. "You have said that you cannot have children, so there will be no other Keepers. If her prophecy holds true, it must be you—and the timing is about right."

"We seem to spend a lot of our time dealing with 'ifs' and 'maybes,'" I said, sighing.

"We do," Simon said, his fingers playing absently with

the necklace he wore. "It is the . . . nature of our task. Not knowing anything for certain, but having . . . faith that what we do know or what we learn will sustain us."

"That doesn't mean I have to like it . . . or even want it. The Boards say I have no choice, but what else would they say? They want whatever this 'opening of the way' is, and have for thousands of years." I caught movement out of the corner of my eye and saw that a number of the stray dogs I'd seen yesterday were gathering near Amber, pausing as if to check on her, and then moving quickly on. It was a strange sight.

"No, you don't," Simon said, his voice and gaze faraway. "Let's just figure things out one day at a time, okay?"

I snapped my fingers in front of his nose. "Hello? Earth to Simon? Come in, Simon."

"What?" he said, refocusing on me.

"You aren't really here," I said. "Life and death, multiple Boards, control of the universe, and you're talking about taking things one day at a time? The Simon Monk I know wouldn't be off in his own world at a time like this."

He offered a small smile and shrugged. "I'm sorry, Jenna," he said. "I had an interesting night, too."

"Oh?" I asked. "What happened?"

"I got a phone call," he said. "From Peraud."

It actually took a minute for Simon's words to sink in, and I just sat there, my cappuccino halfway to my mouth, staring at him. Several words tried to come at once, and I cleared my throat. "Peraud . . . called you?" I finally managed.

Simon nodded. "Yes, he did. He wants to meet with me."

"But why?" I asked. "Why would you even talk to him?"

"He says he knows why we look alike. He knew our parents," Simon said. "He says he wants to talk to me . . . as his brother."

"Simon, Peraud is *evil*. He's tried to kill us on at least two occasions. He doesn't want to talk—it's a trick to get you alone so he can destroy you and get to me more easily."

"I don't think so, Jenna," Simon said. "I'm an orphan—and so is he. He believes we are identical twins, separated at birth." He lifted the coin necklace up and stared at it. "He even has one of these, exactly the same as mine. I know it *could* be a trap, but I still want to know more. He says he knows who our parents were and what happened to them."

Oh boy, I thought. My parents had died when I was little, so I knew what it meant to want to know them. To hold them and be held by them. My last living relative, my grandfather, had died just before I found the Board of the Winds—his death, in fact, had been what started the whole chain of events—and I'd do anything to sit and talk with him for even five minutes now.

"I understand what you're saying, Simon. I really do. I understand your feelings—"

"Then you'll understand why I have to do this," he said. "I've agreed to see him."

"No, Simon," I said. "You can't, you mustn't. Even if you and Peraud *are* twins and he knows your mother and father and has dinner with them every Sunday, you can't. He only wants the power of the Boards for himself." I reached across the table and took his hand. "It's a *trap*, Simon."

"It could be," he admitted, gently pulling his hand away from mine. "And that's why you won't be coming along. You'll stay here with Dario and continue learning how to control the Boards. If it is a trick, the most Peraud will gain is my death—and that's not much of a gain. It's you and the Boards he truly wants. My death wouldn't serve much purpose."

The server started to stop by the table, and I waved him off. "Except making it easier to get to me. And he'd already have me—if it weren't for you."

"You are much more capable now, Jenna," Simon said. "You proved that in Petra when you mastered the Board of the Waters so quickly and used both Boards to save our lives."

And he was right about that part, I knew. With each passing day, I grew more and more comfortable using the power of the Boards. I could protect myself now, but that wasn't the real issue. "And what about me?" I asked, hating the sound of fear and despair in my voice. "What would happen to me if I lost you, too?"

Simon leaned forward and captured my gaze with his storm-blue eyes. "You are very kind, Jenna," he said. "But I don't think you're going to lose me. And if you did, you would go on."

I shook my head. "No, Simon, please. Please don't do this. I . . . I care about you and you know that. You know how I feel, and even if you can't admit you feel it too—"

"Jenna, I know how you feel," he said. "I care about you as well, but my relationship with God and the Church prohibits me from acting on those feelings in the same way another man would. I don't want to keep you from finding real love that can be returned to you."

Damn it, now is not the time for you to be noble! I felt hot tears in my eyes and dashed them away. "How *do* you feel about me, Simon?" I asked. "How do you really feel?"

Simon stared at me for a long moment, then rose and put a handful of euros on the table to pay for our breakfast. "I've got to go," he said. "I'll be back as soon as I can."

"Simon, don't," I said. "Please, let's just talk about this a bit more."

I felt a cold nose press into my hand, and I looked

down to see Amber's golden eye staring at me. She whined softly.

"I have to, Jenna," he said. "Right now, Peraud is the only link to my past, maybe even my family." He slid his arms into his coat. "Dario already knows about this. He's waiting for you and your new friend to come over this morning."

I saw that nothing was going to change his mind— not my feelings and certainly not my tears. He was committed to this course of action, even if it meant his death. I was tempted to call on the Boards, to create a storm that would stop traffic in the streets and blot out the sky with its power. To call a wind that would knock over lampposts and mailboxes and keep everyone indoors, to bring on snow or sleet or ice that would coat every surface, making movement impossible. But I did none of these things. Instead, I decided to let him know *exactly* how I felt.

"So, that's it, then?" I asked. "You're the one who got me into this whole mess with the Boards, and now, because it's no longer convenient for your wants, off you go. That's fine, Simon. In fact, it's just about perfect. Go ahead and commit suicide and leave me here to pick up the pieces and try to figure the rest of this out." I pointed down the street. "Go, damn you! Just go!"

I expected him to argue or try to make his point, and Simon opened his mouth several times to say something, then closed it again with an audible snap. Finally, he stepped forward and wrapped me in a tight hug. "I care about you, Jenna," he whispered into my ear. "But I have to do this. I'll come back safe, and as soon as I can." He squeezed me tighter, then added, "I promise."

Then he let me go, and before I could say another word, he turned and began walking down the street.

A part of me wanted to cry, but I held it in, more angry than hurt. Simon had been with me every day since my whole world had become enveloped in this craziness. And now he wasn't.

I sat down again and ordered another cappuccino. Suddenly, I felt a shove against my thigh and looked down into the golden gaze of Amber. She whined softly, and I scratched behind her ears, which she seemed to enjoy. "Well, at least you're not running off on a fool's errand, are you, girl? Instead, you're stuck with me, which is probably worse."

The morning sunlight had grown stronger, and the day warmed while I finished my breakfast. I paid for the extra drink and stood up. If Simon could go on without me, then I would have to find a way to go on without him. The old saying about loving someone enough to set them free was probably true, and Simon wasn't a fool. He could take care of himself. My heart, however, was going to take a little longer to get used to that idea.

And as for getting the next Board without Simon, I wasn't sure what I was going to do. I could call Armand, but somehow that felt like running for cover. Maybe I needed to do this on my own.

"Come on, Amber," I said, heading down the street. "Dario is waiting."

Pompeii is a city of ghosts and ruins.

In AD 79, it had been completely covered in lava during a massive eruption of Mount Vesuvius that happened so quickly that people died still sitting in their chairs and sleeping in their beds. Their preserved forms, coated in a protective layer of hardened ash and rock, were on display throughout the ruins of their former homes.

It was more than a little disturbing, but there was nothing I could do except try not to look at them.

From the large amphitheatre on one end, where outdoor plays had once been performed, to the *thermae stabianae*, or public baths, the city felt haunted and watched. Much of it had been cleaned up and made presentable for the tourists, but that didn't change its feel. It was a place of cold stones and death, and no amount of sunlight or swept streets would change that.

Dario walked slowly, his hand resting on my arm as he told me about the history of the city. "Vesuvius," he said, "has erupted more than a half dozen times since the Board of the Flames was hidden there by Shalizander's daughter."

"Is the Board causing the eruptions?" I asked, moving around a fallen piece of stone near the ancient amphitheater. It had been two days since Simon left, and my time had been filled with getting to know Dario and learning whatever I could of the Language of the Birds that would help me control the Boards. When I had arrived earlier that morning, Dario had suggested we visit the site of ancient Pompeii, and we had spent most of the day wandering amidst the remains of a civilization preserved for eternity.

While I itched to move on with my search for the Board, I believed that what I had learned so far would be invaluable later. Plus, as Dario constantly stressed to me, as I found and added each new Board to my collection, they would become more and more difficult to control. I *needed* to know as much as possible before moving forward.

"Perhaps," he said, "but it is more likely that the Board's magic is interfering with the natural order of things. I do not know, but I think that when you find the next Board, much will be explained."

"Why do people still live here?" I asked. In the distance, the imposing figure of the mountain was visible, its peak obscured by clusters of low, puffy clouds.

Dario stopped for a moment, looking at the landscape

around us. "The valley is fertile," he said. "The volcanic ash in the soil is actually quite good for growing crops and raising livestock. The people of rural Italy still lead relatively simple lives, compared to much of the world."

"The simple life," I said. "I remember what that used to be like."

The old priest laughed softly. "Yes, I suppose you do." He resumed walking and said, "How are you holding up, young Jenna?"

"What do you mean?" I asked.

He turned toward me, and again, I had the strange feeling that somehow, he was able to see more about me than anyone I'd ever met. "Aside from the fact that Simon is now gone, I meant how are you dealing with the strain the Boards are putting on you?" When I didn't answer right away, he rushed to add, "I apologize. I don't mean to pry or make you uncomfortable. I only mentioned it because the burdens of being the Keeper are many."

"It's okay. One minute, one hour at a time, I suppose," I said, then shook my head as my thoughts turned elsewhere. "Simon shouldn't have left. Peraud can't be trusted."

Dario snorted. "Of course Peraud can't be trusted. Just the same, we *must* trust Simon, and that he knows what is best for himself right now. And you understand, I think, the longing for family."

"I do," I said softly. "And I trust him. It's just that . . . ."

My words trailed off as I tried to think of a way to describe how I felt about Simon, and failed.

"I understand, Jenna," Dario said. "But enough sadness and wondering for now. It's time for us to see how your control with the Boards is progressing." He turned down another ash-coated street, the setting sun casting a long shadow of his bent form on the ground. I hurried to walk beside him. "To the center of the ruins," he added.

"Why?" I asked. "What's there?"

"A test," Dario said. "Difficult, but not impossible. And necessary, if you are truly to master the Board of the Flames and the ones that follow it." He looked at me appraisingly. "You believe you're strong enough to handle the third Board, but I have my doubts. In this way, we shall see."

I wasn't sure what to expect, but in my experience pop quizzes were almost never a good thing.

"My Lord, my plan has worked. I await only your command to move forward."

"Then our friend Simon is out of the way?"

"Completely, my Lord. He can no longer interfere with our goals."

"Excellent, Peraud. You are finally proving that my investment in you was worthwhile."

"Thank you, my Lord. What are your wishes?"

"By all means, continue. It's time we see if the emotional weakness we've observed in the young Keeper is more than an aberration, but a true character flaw."

There are different kinds of darkness, and a night with no moon over the ruins of an ancient city is particularly unnerving. Especially when one is surrounded by roving packs of howling, barking dogs. And ghosts.

Dario had taken me to the very center of what had once been the market in Pompeii. Moss-covered stones unearthed by teams of archeologists lay here and there, left where they had been found. Not far away, the remains of several long-dead citizens were kept on public display for the tourists, frescoes of posed death. It was macabre and disturbing, and felt like sitting in a cemetery where the dead rested uneasily.

Which in Pompeii, they did.

"The dogs, you understand," Dario told me before he left, "are much more than just trapped souls. They are the guardians of Pompeii—or so some of the more ancient legends say. They linger here, and their howls are supposed to serve as a warning to the citizens that a Keeper has returned to their city."

"But no one remembers that?" I asked.

Dario shook his head. "Some legends are forgotten because to tell them is too horrible." He grasped my arm. "It's up to you, Jenna, to assure them that you do not mean any harm, but in fact, wish only to *remove* the Board of the Flames," he added. "For they will find you after nightfall, and then you must confront them."

"And how will I convince them of that?" I asked.

"I do not know," he said. "But you are the Keeper of the Boards, and you will have their powers to guide and protect you."

"I don't even know all their powers yet!" I objected. "I haven't even had a chance to *start* learning how they work."

"You have been given everything you need," he said, patting me on the arm. "You'll do just fine."

"You have more confidence in me than I do," I said.

"Jenna, long ago, many of the Keepers had magic of their own, aside from the abilities the Boards gave them. It appears that those powers have died out in your line, though your great-grandmother Marissa had some skills in that area. That said, the Boards are powerful in their own right, and their limits have yet to be explored. The best way to learn about them is by using them and mastering them constantly—not to open yourself up to their evil influence, but to master their essences for the purposes of good. Here is a chance to do just that. The spirits of Pompeii have been restless for centuries. It is time for them to rest."

His words had reminded me uncomfortably of what Saduj had said, and I struggled to accept them. Still, I had to trust Dario—there was no one else for me to rely on anymore. As though sensing my decision, he had given me another pat on the arm and walked away, leaning on a staff and looking for all the world like a man who had the utmost confidence in what he'd just done.

"Wait, aren't you going to at least stay and help me?" I had called after him. "Is this really important?"

Dario had turned back and slowly shaken his head. "You don't understand yet, young Jenna. This is something only you can do—and you must do it, or we'll never reach the Board of the Flames. The spirits guard more than just the city." And with that, he was gone, and I was left alone to wait with only the dogs and my growing worries for company.

Nightfall came all too swiftly for my taste, but there was little I could do. If Dario thought this experience was a necessary test of my abilities, then I had to try. So far, everything he taught me had been worthwhile, especially the various words in the Language of the Birds that I used to command and control the Boards. When I'd asked him where he'd learned it, he smiled, the wrinkles around his eyes growing deeper as he recalled the memory.

"Marissa and I tricked the Board of the Winds into teaching her the words over a period of several months," he'd said. "We developed lines of questioning on innocuous words and phrases and figured out the important words one at a time." Laughing, he added, "The Board was *not* happy when we tested the words for the first time."

"No, Keeper, I was not," the Board of the Winds had

hissed in my mind. *"Those are words that belonged to another time and place and to true sorcerers of power."*

I had told Dario what the Board said, and he had chuckled softly. "Never forget, Jenna, that despite their strange form, the Boards are entities in their own right—they have feelings and thoughts and plans of their own, any or all of which may or may not be the same as yours. They are tricky and willing to deceive you to accomplish what they want, so *never* lose sight of the fact that you must always be their master—or else they will master you."

Over the last two days, we'd talked about a lot of things, and I felt better than I had in weeks about my role as the Keeper of the Boards. Though limited in his knowledge and abilities, Dario was a wonderful mentor, guiding me while also letting me reach my own understanding about how the Boards operated. And while I still wasn't sure how I was going to handle it all, at least I was a bit better equipped to do so now. At least I thought I was, until the spirits began to approach me on the far side of the stone square.

At first, they appeared as wisps of fog, swirling and gray just above the stones. But as I looked closer, I saw that the mist was rising from beneath the stones of the square, and as I watched, it took human shape. One, then two, then so many that I rapidly lost count. The forms twined about each other, soundless and staring, and giving off a luminescent light of their own.

Slowly, the square filled with the spirits until I was surrounded on all sides. I watched as the dogs continued howling and running through the area—all of them except Amber, who sat at my side, unmoving even as the spirits began to close in on us.

It was then that I realized I could *hear* them. The sounds they made were not vocal, but were in my head, much like the voices of the Boards.

"She is a Keeper . . . ."

"A Keeper has come . . . ."

"No, she is only a Holder, the line of Keepers is long since dead."

"She is a Keeper; I can feel it in her blood."

"Taste her spirit. That will tell us!"

When they started talking about blood and tasting my spirit, I felt a chill slide up my spine. I called on the Boards in my backpack.

"Bring forth a wind," I said. *"Blow these ghosts back to whatever world they came from."*

"No wind will touch them, Keeper," the Board of the Winds replied.

"Nor rain or ice or snow," the Board of the Waters added.

"They are not of this world and are untouchable by our powers," they said in unison.

Untouchable?

"At all?" I asked. *"There is nothing you can do?"*

"We may command the elements and entities tied to the elements. The spirits of Pompeii walk the land of the dead. They are beyond us, and do not fear our powers."

"Now what do I do?" I asked.

The Board of the Winds said, *"Previous Keepers would have used their own magical abilities to defend themselves from such an attack."*

"As it is, we are both curious to see what you are going to do here as well," the Board of the Waters added.

Cold, stinging fingers caressed my arm, and I looked up to see that the spirits had closed me in on all sides, swirling around me and reaching out to touch me with dozens of spectral hands. The chill went all the way to the bone, and even though the night was balmy, my teeth chattered as shivers ran up my body.

At my feet, Amber watched the spirits intently, and as another closed on me, she barked once, loud and sharp, and it backed away.

"Good girl," I said, thinking that I was going to have to come up with something better than a barking dog, and fast.

As I watched, the spirits parted to reveal a more detailed figure. The outline of flowing robes and ancient jewelry were clearly visible over a broad-shouldered masculine form. Perhaps a priest from long ago. It spoke in my mind, a voice of power and ice. *"What do you want here, Keeper?"*

Answering in the same way I spoke to the Boards, I said, *"I wish only to pass this way, to retrieve the Board of the Flames and take it far from this place."*

"Yet you bring two more Boards with you," the spirit said. *"They are evil, and those who carry them are evil as well. It was a Keeper that brought about our destruction, and the magic of the Board that keeps us here—trapped for all eternity."*

I wasn't quite sure what else I might say to convince him that I meant no harm, but Amber barked again and shoved her nose into my hand, which I decided must mean to keep trying. *"The first Board was awakened by mistake, setting off the chain that will awaken the others. The Boards* must *be found by me, else they will be found by others whose intentions we do not know. Would you have me judge you based on* your *ancestors?"* I asked.

Wrong question. All around me the spirits shrieked, and for a second I thought my brain would simply explode.

"Our ancestors were traders and merchants and winemakers. They harmed no one and lived their lives in peace," the spirit said. *"To be judged by one's ancestors should be a great honor, and for us it would be. For you, I fear, it would not."*

It wasn't going well, and the gathered spirits were circling closer and closer.

"I want only to take the Board of the Flames away from here, never to return," I said. *"Isn't the Board what caused all your problems in the first place? I'd think you would be glad to have it gone!"*

"We have no choice but to guard the Board, Keeper. Should you fail our test, you will not be allowed to continue your quest."

I heard the sound of a threat in his words, and responded, *"Very well, in what way would you test me? I am the last Keeper of the Boards, the Daughter of Destiny as foretold by Shalizander. I must pass your test and retrieve the Board, or else all that has gone before is lost."*

"Our test, Keeper, is simple," he said. His ghostly arms rose to take in the hundreds of spirits around him. *"You have but to find a way to defeat all of us, and our promise will be fulfilled."*

"You are spirits," I said. *"I am flesh. You cannot harm me, nor can you stand against the magic of the Boards."*

"We shall see, Keeper," he said. *"I sense a great evil around you, a cloud of shadow. Like the one who first brought the Board of the Flames here, and the one who looked like you that came here many years later. All Keepers are surrounded by evil and seek only power. You must be destroyed before your foul magic brings even more ruin upon us!"*

The spirit faded back into the whirling dance of the others, his form disappearing and reappearing like a flickering light.

Amber began barking excitedly, and the spirits continued their dance. Writhing and twisting, they spun closer and closer, and I was reminded of the fire elementals—only instead of burning, these creatures would freeze my body and drag my soul into whatever realm they inhabited.

"Ideas?" I asked the Boards.

"As we have said, they are spirits, Keeper, and not subject to harm from the elements," the Board of the Waters replied. If I hadn't known any better, I could have sworn the Board's voice contained a note of petulance. *Fat lot of help they are now.*

As the spirits continued their dance, I found myself ducking and dodging, trying to keep their outstretched arms from touching my skin. I wasn't positive, but I felt that allowing them to touch me—despite my boast—would be harmful, if not fatal.

Amber continued to bark, and soon the other dogs took up the chorus. To any observer, it would have been a haunting scene—ghostly white forms spinning and dancing to the music of howling and barking dogs. To me, it was simply terrifying.

"Call the winds!" I ordered the Board of the Winds, thinking that anything was better than nothing. A

ghostly hand caressed my shoulder, and an icy chill sent a spasm through my muscles. *"Now!"*

"No wind will avail you, Keeper," the Board replied with a finality that made me shudder.

I was on my own, and other than an excitable German shepherd, had few options for help.

"Back off! I don't want to hurt you!" I cast the thought at the ghosts, but their only reply was mocking laughter and taunts.

"She lies! She lies!"

"She has no magic of her own!"

"Touch her flesh. Let her feel how forever cold it is here."

"How very cold . . . ."

The spirits whirled closer and closer, and only by dodging and spinning could I keep them from touching me. I knew that I'd quickly exhaust myself, but I didn't have any choice. I tried to glimpse a path through them, a way out of the square, but in every direction, a wall of writhing forms blocked my way.

An icy hand gripped my wrist and I felt my arm go numb as I yanked it away.

A strong pair of hands shoved me from behind, and my spine stiffened as I stumbled forward.

Another ghostly form caught me, and up close I could see that its face was only a grinning skull. Terrified, I screamed as it kissed my cheek and pushed me away, my facial muscles frozen from the touch.

Panting and out of breath, I stumbled and went to my knees. My whole body felt numb, and I knew that even getting to my feet would be painful. *Where the hell is Simon when I need him?* I thought. Looking up, I saw the spirits moving closer, reaching out for me.

Without any other options, I drew a deep breath to begin screaming for help when I remembered something the spirit priest had said. Something about a promise being fulfilled. *"Wait!"* I called. *"You spoke of a promise ! Is this how you fulfill an oath?"*

Several of the spirits screamed, and they started backing away. The priest reappeared, his figure forming from the mists. *"Are you calling on us to fulfill our oath?"* his voice rang in my mind, a note of curiosity in his tone.

"What is your oath?"

A sound like a collective sigh passed through the gathered spirits.

"We are bound to an order of protection."

"What are you supposed to protect?" I asked.

"Should the final heir to Shalizander come, one of us is bound to protect her, and should she succeed, we will be released."

Amber barked once, as if confirming that she was my protector.

"I am Shalizander's heir! I already told you that."

"Some here believe that; some do not. We seek proof of your claim."

"What kind of proof?" I asked. *"I am who I am."*

"It was foretold to us that you would come bringing a sign of true faith."

"I don't understand."

"And that is why you will fail our test. That is why, Keeper, you will die."

Amber began growling again, snapping as the spirits closed in once more. I noticed that they tried to avoid her snapping jaws, and did not attempt to harm her. If I could've, I would have wrapped her around me like a blanket.

Getting to my feet, my whole body aching, I began backing away. I spun around, hoping to see a way out or some sign of help, but there was nothing and no one. I continued moving away from the spirits, until I found myself leaning against the central stone in the square. Amber leaned against my legs, barking and growling.

I had failed Dario's test, but for all the wrong reasons. I believed in God, but could not produce any signs of true faith. Not without Simon . . . . *He* was my sign of true faith.

The spirits continued moving closer, occasionally brushing by me, sending an icy spike into my bones. Their misty limbs drifted out to caress my skin, and I felt goose bumps break out all over my body, only to have the warmth of my blood cause them to disappear again. Panicked, I turned and felt one of the wraiths pass directly through me.

I gasped for air, even as I felt my heart stop beating, frozen in place as though my blood had turned to liquid nitrogen. I couldn't breathe, couldn't move, and then it passed and I managed a weak breath. I was going to die, and I knew it. I stumbled and found myself on my knees again, wrapping my arms around Amber's warmth. My jaws ached from my chattering teeth and my lungs moved, but it felt like I was drowning in the cold.

I couldn't speak and began to feel myself float away, looking down on myself and on the spirits at though I was no longer a part of the scene itself.

A sudden burst of light dawned over the square, and a strong voice called out, "Begone!" There was a booming sound like a thunderclap, and I felt my body jolted by the shock wave. I was no longer looking down at the scene, but trapped—voiceless and without the ability to even move—inside my half-frozen body. The ghostly dancers stopped immediately and began retreating from the form entering the courtyard.

In the bright light, I couldn't see who it was.

"Begone, spirits!" the voice called again. "Return to the realm from which you came!"

The form moved closer, calling once again for the spirits to depart, and I recognized Simon's voice. I wanted to call out to him, but I didn't have the breath to do so. My lungs felt like chunks of ice embedded in my chest.

"Jenna!" he said, closing the final distance between us. He knelt next to me and shook his head. His coin necklace spun in slow, hypnotic circles, changing from bright to dark and back again.

The spirits moved farther away, but hadn't departed completely yet. "Hang on, Jenna," Simon said, squeezing my hand. "Stay with me just a minute longer."

I watched, unable to speak or move as he stood, taking a large, golden crucifix out of his waist pack and holding it up overhead. It glowed with a light of its own. In his loud, clear, wonderful-sounding voice, Simon chanted words in what sounded like Latin, which I knew almost nothing of except *carpe diem* and *e pluribus unum*.

Whatever he said, it was working, because the spirits screamed in my mind, gibbering in true fear, and began dispersing. Their pallid forms slipped back into the stones at our feet, and their cries faded almost as rapidly as they did.

"Paenitens diabolus stetit sensitque quam dira sit probitas!" Simon said, his deep voice carrying in the night air.

A sign of true faith, I thought.

A final shriek rent the night air, and it was then I realized the sound wasn't coming from the spirits but from the dogs, who ran all around the ruins, yowling at the top of their lungs. As the last spirits disappeared, so did they—all except Amber, who sat at my feet, panting and tired.

Simon knelt down near me once more, then placed his lips over mine. I felt air—glorious warm air—fill my lungs. "Come on, Jenna," he whispered. "Breathe!" Again, then again, his warm lips touched mine, and he breathed into me.

Finally, I was able to draw a gasping breath. It felt like fire searing my lungs from the inside out, but the pain was nothing. I was alive . . . and I owed my life to Simon. Shivering, I stuttered, "Th-thanks."

"Don't try to talk right now," he said. He pulled off his coat and wrapped it around me. "You'll feel better once you've warmed up some. The spirits' touch manifests physically, but the damage shouldn't be permanent." He rubbed my arms and legs briskly, and I felt the shivering subside a little.

"What did you say to them?" I asked him once my teeth had stopped chattering enough to speak.

He took my hands and helped me to my feet, wrapping me in his strong arms. "They are *mors aeterna*, never-ending death, and it would be wrong to speak more of it," he said. "The spirits of the dead can kill with their touch. I . . . I nearly lost you." He held me tighter, and I felt the warmth of his breath on my neck as he stroked my hair and back with one hand. "I can't . . . couldn't imagine losing you," he whispered.

I felt so glad to be close to his living warmth, so close to him, that I felt a smile cross my lips.

"I'm fine," I said. "I just feel stupid." I looked more closely at him, and smiled. "And a little stunned. I didn't expect to see you again anytime soon."

"My meeting with Peraud was shorter than I expected," he said. His words were clipped of emotion.

"Are *you* okay?" I asked him. "What happened at your meeting?"

"Of course," he said. "I told you I'd be fine." He pulled me closer and gave me one final squeeze before releasing me. "I'm sorry to have worried you, Jenna," he said, staring into my eyes earnestly. "Let's get out of here. It was unwise for Dario to test you this way."

I started to give him his coat back, but he shook his head. "Keep it. I'm warm enough for now."

Discouraged and angry at myself for failing, I asked, "What did he think would happen? The Boards said they have no power over the spirits of the dead."

"He may have believed that an attack by something like the spirits might bring out any latent magical abilities you have," Simon said. "*If* you had them, which you don't. That ability appears to have disappeared from your family at least a generation or two ago."

"The spirits said something about a promise," I said.

"To protect Shalizander's final heir if she showed a sign of true faith."

Simon laughed grimly. "Well, they got that anyway."

We walked out of the ruins and back down the narrow street to the café across from our hotel. We didn't speak much, but Simon held my hand the whole way, and I wondered what his meeting with Peraud had done to him. He seemed more like himself than he had in a long time, relaxed and confident. It was also amazing to watch him use his priestly abilities with such conviction. Simon was clearly a man of God.

But the way he'd held me, breathed life into me, protected me . . . it was what I had wanted, what I ached for. To be in Simon's arms was a dream fulfilled.

And yet . . . I was destined to be the Keeper of the Boards, and it was clear that Simon believed he was destined to be a priest.

For us to be denied the possibility of love on top of everything else was one blow too many. Surely even Simon would understand that.

We were meant to be together, no matter what.

I realized that I was still holding Simon's hand at the same time he realized that he was still holding mine. Unspoken words and unanswered questions hovered like spirits in the air between us, but some silences are too fragile to break, and neither of us said a word.

* * *

Considering the ache in my heart, I slept well that night, with Amber at my feet and the Board's voices more quiet than normal. If I had dreams, for once they did not disturb or awaken me, and when I woke the next morning, I was more rested than I had been in weeks, and was profoundly grateful. After another breakfast of hard rolls and a cappuccino, Simon and I made our way to Dario's house.

I wanted to know how Simon's meeting with Peraud went, but he seemed deep in thought as we walked along the old streets, and I was hesitant to disturb him. The man could be as mysterious as anything we were dealing with, but knowing what had happened was too important to be put off.

"So," I said, "are you going to tell me about it, or will I have to read it in your diary?"

"About what?" Simon muttered, his voice faraway.

I cleared my throat. "The meeting with Peraud?"

Simon glanced up at me and shrugged. "It was nothing, really. He thinks we're identical twins, abandoned by our parents and separated at birth. He was found at an orphanage in Paris, which is where he grew up."

"So how did he get involved with the Templars?" I asked. "What are his plans now that he thinks or knows you two are brothers?" I had a hundred questions on the tip of my tongue.

"Always curious, aren't you, Jenna?" Simon asked. "I

learned a few important things. Peraud found his 'faction' of the Templars at about the same time Armand got involved—but the fracturing of the organization goes back much further than that, to some other sorcerer, whose name he didn't know."

"Or didn't want to tell you," I interrupted. "He can't be trusted."

Ignoring me, Simon continued on. "He also mentioned . . . ."

"What?" I asked when his words trailed off.

"That our mother is still alive," he finished. "He said that he found her, living in London, a few years ago."

"Oh my God," I whispered. "So . . . you have family. That's wonderful news!" I put my hand on his arm. "What are you going to do?"

"I'm not sure yet," he said. "Perhaps I'll look her up when I have the courage, get more information. Peraud *could* be lying about all this."

"You should talk to her," I said. "Maybe there's a good reason why she gave you up for adoption."

"Maybe," Simon said. "But she didn't get to spend those years in an orphanage—I did—and it's going to be a while before I'm ready to face her. Just knowing that she's alive is a good thing, though."

"I understand. Did Peraud say anything else?" I asked.

Simon shook his head. "It was a short meeting. He

didn't say much else except that he would stay out of our way. That's one threat eliminated, anyway."

"And you believed him?" I asked. "Just like that? That you're twins and everything is fine and dandy?"

"Peraud is capable of telling any lie that suits his desires, and this could be one of them, but I don't think so." He paused, then added, "Yes, I believe him."

"Why?"

"What purpose would lying serve him in this instance?"

"I don't know, but since when do we trust someone so obviously evil?"

Simon was quiet for a moment, then said, "Evil?" He shook his head. "I think he's very . . . misguided, Jenna. I've spent my life surrounded by the good men of the Church. He wasn't so lucky, and we've traveled very different paths. I don't know for sure what Peraud is really up to, but for now I'm inclined to believe him."

Well, we didn't know what he was up to, that much was certain. Still, I had the feeling that there were some things Simon wasn't saying. But I knew he'd tell me in his own time. Trying to find out anything more before he was ready to talk was as pointless as arguing with a statue.

We kept our silence the rest of the way to Dario's house. The old priest was up and waiting, opening the door before we could even knock.

"Come in, Jenna, come in," he said. "Good morning. I trust your test went well?"

"No, it didn't," I said. But before I could launch into a full-scale rant, Dario interrupted.

"Simon?" he asked. "I'm surprised to see you back so soon."

"He came back last night," I said. "If he hadn't, I'd have died in that little test of yours."

Ignoring me completely, Dario kept his attention on Simon. "Are you well?" he asked.

"Yes," Simon said, sounding irritated. "I'm perfectly fine. Perhaps we can focus on this so-called test you put Jenna up to."

"I . . . ." Dario began to say, then shook his head, leaving the thought incomplete.

Simon cleared his throat. "Why would you choose to test Jenna that way?" he asked, his voice sharp. "She nearly died!"

"I thought . . . ." Dario's words trailed off, and he shook his head. "Jenna, I'm sorry," he said. "I shouldn't have done it. . . . It just . . . . I'd hoped it would bring out your latent magical abilities."

"Who are you to put the Keeper of the Boards through such a trial?" Simon demanded. "She has enough dangers to face without you adding to them!" He actually took a step forward, and I put a restraining hand on his arm.

"Simon, that's enough," I said quietly. "Dario has done nothing but try to help me."

"I *am* sorry, Jenna," Dario said, his lined face cracking with sadness. "Truly. I only thought . . . . Well, it doesn't matter what I thought. Simon is right. I needlessly put in you danger. Please forgive me."

I stepped forward and embraced him in a hug. He tensed, surprised and uncertain, then hugged me back.

"There is nothing to forgive," I said. Though I had been furious with him last night and even a little this morning, there was no point in making him feel worse than he already did. Besides that, even though he hadn't known *why* it was necessary, the more I thought about it, the more I felt like my encounter with the spirits was important. And if it got me to the next Board a little faster, that was even better.

"Thank you," Dario said when we separated.

"Well, then, unless you have any other tests or teachings up your sleeve, I have an idea," Simon said.

"No, nothing," the old man said quickly.

"What did you have in mind, Simon?" I asked.

"I thought maybe we'd do a little scouting around the outskirts of the ruins," he said. "There are some small villas near the vineyards, and the people that live here have long memories, with stories sometimes going back thousands of years. Perhaps we will be able to find a

JENNA SOLITAIRE

clue as to how Shalizander's daughter got into Vesuvius to hide the Board."

"A good idea," Dario seconded. "And, after last night, a day of exploring and relaxation is in order."

"Then we're all agreed," I said. "Where do we start?"

102

"Peraud?"

"My Lord?"

"Your personal ambitions may prove to be your undoing."

"I . . . I live only to serve you, my Lord."

"Of course you do. All the same, consider yourself warned. Our pawns in this game must remain unaware, and you must exercise extreme caution. Their ignorance is crucial. My plans must unfold as I wish. Do not jeopardize them for any reason, least of all to fulfill your own petty desires."

"As you command, my Lord."

The outskirts of Pompeii were mostly vineyards and small farms, interspersed with the ruins of ancient buildings that had been long abandoned and overgrown. We started out our day near the ancient amphitheater, following old trails and waving to the occasional *tourista* as we passed. Several times, we stopped to talk to winemakers in the region, most of whom had families that had been in the region for generations. Unfortunately, none of them could offer stories that would help our quest.

Shortly before lunch, we came upon a jumble of boulders near a small inn. The inn itself was unremarkable—a small, wooden structure with a porch facing the mountains. I tried not to be bothered by the fact that the meat available on the menu—lamb—was running around in holding pens in the back of the building. We ordered lunch—fresh salads, fruit and bread, as well as meats and cheese—and took all of it outside to enjoy in the sunshine.

We were sitting amongst the boulders when Simon suddenly stopped eating and pointed at an upthrust stone. "Jenna! Take a look at that," he said.

I was distracted with trying to feed Amber, who had kept her distance all day and was obviously uncomfortable about something, and he repeated my name several times before I turned away from the dog in disgust.

"She won't eat," I said. "Not even the meat."

"Never mind the dog," Simon said. "Come look at this." He crouched next to the finger of stone and brushed moss off the surface.

I knelt next to him, ignoring Amber's plaintive whine. "What is it?" I asked.

"Look at the markings," he said. "They are the same as, or very similar to, the runes on the Boards."

I peered closer and nodded, feeling excitement course through my veins. "Yes," I said. "Almost exactly."

Removing my backpack, I pulled the now-combined Boards of Air and Water out. The runes on the Board of the Waters had three matches: an inverted V shape with three wavy lines above it, two rows of small circles with a series of lines between them, and a cloud-shaped rune. The first one looked like a representation of a volcano or maybe fire from the earth, the second a river, and the third seemed self-explanatory. I pointed them out to Simon, and he nodded.

I turned to Dario and asked, "What do they mean?"

"The Language of the Birds is *not* the language of magic," he said. "They are like . . . cousins. The difference between old Latin and Spanish. Similar in some ways, of course, but not the same." He thought about it for a moment, then said, "Perhaps the order of the symbols is meaningful."

"From top to bottom, there's a volcano, then the river, and then the cloud," I said. "Your guess is as good as mine."

Dario laughed. "It's a warning."

"A warning of what?" Simon asked.

"To stay on the far side of water when the volcano is erupting," Dario replied.

"Then what's the cloud shape?" I asked.

"Steam," Simon said. "Superheated water from the lava flows creates steam."

"And all of this is helpful how?" I asked, trying and failing to keep the sarcasm out of my voice. "What kind of a clue is this?"

"Maybe it's not," Simon said. "Perhaps Shalizander's daughter left it to warn people."

I shook my head. "No, I don't think so. Malizander was running for her life after she left the Board of the Flames here. She wouldn't have had time to do anything this elaborate."

Thankfully, Simon didn't bother to ask how I knew that. He had finally reached a point where he accepted my dreams and visions as accurate, if not always relevant, information.

"Then why is the stone here?" he asked. "How many other people could have made those marks?"

"There have been many Keepers over the years," Dario said. "And many enemies of the Keepers. To us, a hundred years is a long time. In the span of recorded human history, it is the blink of an eye."

"You're being cryptic for no reason," Simon said.

"Not at all, young man," Dario said. "From what

106

Marissa and I learned, the early Keepers were sorcerers and lived extended life spans."

"And?" I asked.

"And what if," he asked, "Malizander was here more than once?"

We fell silent, knowing that Dario had probably hit upon exactly what had happened. So why, I wondered, had she come back? And when? These questions that I knew were probably answered in the pages of Chronicle.

"Where are we staying tonight?" I asked.

"There is a villa near here that offers rooms and food," Simon said. "I looked it up in the tour book earlier. Why?"

"I need a place to stop and read the Chronicle," I said. "That's the only way of finding out what we need to know."

"Jenna . . . ." Simon began, but I cut him off.

"You know I'm right, Simon," I said. "And if she did come here more than once, there had to have been a *good* reason. We need to know what it was."

He sighed. "Fair enough. Let's get you to someplace where you can rest afterward. Maybe what Dario has taught you will help with the effect that reading it has on you."

"Maybe," I said. "But even if it doesn't, what choice do we have?"

"There is always a choice," Dario said. "It's just not always a good one."

"That about sums it up," I said, rising to my feet and putting the Boards away. "Let's get going."

We gathered our belongings and followed Simon down the road, my new friend Amber bringing up the rear and looking for all the world like she wanted to be somewhere else.

At that moment, I knew exactly how she felt.

It was midafternoon by the time we reached the villa and checked in. It was a friendly, family-owned place, with several children of various ages running here and there and at least three generations of relatives helping run the place. The villa sprawled over an acre or two, and encompassed a restaurant and tavern, a vineyard, and several different types of livestock. In a way, it was like stepping back through time, though I did notice that they offered satellite television and wireless Internet access. *Two of the comforts of home, at least*, I thought.

It wasn't the past, but it wore a good disguise.

Simon escorted me to my room and offered to stay with me while I read the Chronicle, but I shook my head.

"No, thanks," I said. "I wouldn't be able to concentrate. Why don't you and Dario go explore the villa? This place looks like it's been here a thousand years."

Simon laughed. "It practically has. The lady at the desk told me that the family has been here for at least nine generations."

"I'm not surprised," I said. "I thought the television and the Internet were nice touches, though."

"Even in the most rural of places, technology eventually makes its mark," Simon said. "It is, I think, a kind of magic."

"I don't know if it's magic," I said, "but if I can check my e-mail, I'm a lot happier."

"I'm sure," Simon said, his eyes never leaving mine. "I'll leave you to your reading. Just remember to try to get some rest, too."

"Thanks, I will," I said, watching him shut the door.

Amber chose a place at the foot of the bed, and once again I wondered at her strange behavior. She'd latched onto me in Pompeii, and followed me everywhere, ignoring or even appearing to avoid direct contact with Simon and Dario. Maybe it was because he'd banished those spirits, which Dario said were also in the dogs themselves. That could certainly explain her skittishness. I locked the door and curled up in a comfortable, overstuffed chair, setting my backpack on the floor beside me.

I removed the Boards, which had been quiet since yesterday, not even talking to each other, and the Chronicle, while making a mental note to check e-mail later on.

"Do you know why Malizander came here?" I asked the Board of the Winds. *"Did she come here more than once?"*

"The daughter of Shalizander came here to hide our brother, the Board of the Flames, within the heart of Mount Vesuvius," the Board of the Winds hissed in my mind. *"I journeyed with her, as you know."*

"Did she come here again?" I asked.

"Not while I was in her possession," the Board replied. *"It is possible she came after her daughter had taken the mantle of Keeper."*

I remembered what Dario had said about the Boards, and wondered . . . . *"Are you lying to me?"* I asked.

The Board of the Winds laughed in my mind, a sibilant hiss that tickled my scalp. *"We serve a common cause, Keeper. What purpose would there be in hiding such trivial information from you?"*

"I don't know," I admitted. *"But I don't trust you."*

"You will learn to trust us," the Board of the Waters interjected. *"You will have no choice, should you wish to survive the ordeals to come and be the one to open the way."*

"Trust between the Keeper and the Boards is paramount," the Board of the Winds added. *"Only then can*

our full powers be utilized. Only then will the way be opened."

I wasn't sure if I believed that or not. It didn't feel like they trusted me, and trusting them didn't feel like an option.

Choosing not to ask questions that would only be answered in riddles again, I set the Boards aside and held the Chronicle in my lap. Reading the ancient journal was always a daunting task, because once I started on a passage, I *became* the person who had written it, experiencing the events as though I was living them. When the passage was finished, I would be disoriented and sick, sometimes *very* sick, and extremely tired. It was like running a marathon without any water the day after a twenty-four–hour flu bug. Worse still, the experiences journaled by previous Keepers were rarely pleasant, and were often disturbing.

Opening the Chronicle, feeling its chill on my skin, I paged forward, skimming and doing my best to ignore the brief passages that flittered through my mind as I read them, seeking to draw me in. . . .

. . . Run! Run as though your very life depends on it! . . .

. . . Look at them . . . thousands and thousands of locusts. . . .

. . . That Board is not a brother, but a sister. . . .

"Where are you, Malizander?" I said to myself. "Talk to me."

And then my eyes lit on her name, and once more, I was taken away to another place, to be someone else . . . maybe someone I had been long ago.

The city is gone. Its amphitheater, baths, courtyards, and people are all buried under tons of ash and molten lava now hardened to rock. In time, dirt will cover the rock, and then it will be as if they never existed at all.

I walk past where the children once played in the streets and make my way into the devastated country-side. Here and there, smoke still lingers, rising from the superheated ground. High above, clouds cover the last plumes of ash, rising from the top of the volcano. I killed them all—every man, woman, and child—to ensure that those who followed me, who hunted the Board of the Flames, would die, too.

Shuddering, I walk on. Far behind me, the ship and its crew wait in the harbor. They fear this place, after seeing what happened here, and will not come ashore. Looking around the barren landscape, the lost vine-yards, the feel of the place—like a mass grave . . . I cannot blame them.

I did this, and I know that it will haunt me for the rest of my days.

The volcano shudders once more, and the ground tilts

beneath my feet. The Earth itself is unhappy, and I wonder how long it will take until it calms down and order is restored. Then I remember something my mother once told me, that the Boards are entities of Chaos, constrained by the Order of magic. I think the Earth will never rest easy so long as they exist.

Ahead, I see an upthrust finger of stone. It looks like a road marker, but it will serve my purpose well enough. There are no roads left here, and it will be some years before people return and establish new vineyards and farms on this soil. There are too many memories here now, too many ghosts.

"Is that what you are seeking, Keeper?" a voice I do not recognize asks in my head.

I look around, but there is no one here but the dead. "Who said that?" I ask.

"Do you seek ghosts? Spirits of those who have left this world for the next?"

At the foot of the stone, a wispy figure emerges, its form barely visible. A spirit.

"I do not seek ghosts," I say. "I seek to lay my own ghosts to rest."

"There can be no rest for one such as you," it replies. "Why have you returned?"

"To leave a warning for those who would come here seeking to plunder the treasure I left in the volcano."

"A pointless activity," it says. "We are here."

I begin to ask who he means, but all around me, the figures of more and more spirits rise from cracks in the ground. A dozen, two dozen, then more and more, so quickly that I lose count. In my mind, they scream in anger, in righteous rage. They are the dead of Pompeii. And I have killed them.

"What do you want of me?" I ask. "I was given no choice in my duty."

"As though you gave us a choice?" the spirit says. "You did not warn us, but ran for the harbor and left us to die. And then the magics unleashed by your cursed Board trapped us here—not of this world, but unable to go to the next!"

"I. . . ." Words fail me, and all I can mutter is, "I did not know."

"Such words should be saved when you face judgment in the next world, Keeper. A lack of knowledge is not an excuse."

Remembering all my mother had taught me, especially to own up to the consequences of what I have done, I nod in agreement.

"You are right," I say. "So what would you have of me?"

"You will work a magic upon this place," it says. "A great magic."

"What?" I ask, feeling a chill in my bones. "There has been magic enough here, I think."

"We wish for you to give us the power to inhabit human bodies," it says.

Stunned, I stare at the apparition. "That's . . . that's an abomination!" I say. "Possession? Has death driven you to madness?"

"We hunger for the warmth of the sun," it says. "To touch, to feel, to love."

"I will not do this for you," I say. "Even if such powers were within my abilities—and they are not—I would not do this. It is wrong."

"You will do this for us, Keeper," it says. "Or we will kiss you with our frozen lips, until your physical body freezes and dies . . . and you become one of us."

I shudder. Spirits of the dead have such powers, should they choose to use them. I look around and realize that as the afternoon sun has gone down, more and more spirits have arrived. I am surrounded, and I left the Board of the Winds back on the ship. I don't want to call on it now—its voice, its powers, even touching its cold surface is difficult for me. The task my mother set before me is sapping my strength.

There are now hundreds of spirits, moaning and wailing in my mind. How many did I kill? How many innocents lost because of my actions?

"I do not have the power to do this," I say. "But there is an alternative."

"What alternative do you suggest?" the spirit asks.

"The power of possession is beyond me, when it applies to human life," I say. "But. . . ."

I reach out with my magical senses. There are still many animals in the area. Having sensed the impending eruption, they fled before it could take their lives, and have already started to return. As if ashamed of their cowardice, many domestic dogs had come home, seeking their lost masters. "There are many dogs in the area. Once they were your pets. With my magic, I can make their bodies available to you."

For long moments, the wailing and screaming of the dead was the only sound I could hear. Then, the spirit spoke. "Yes, this is acceptable to us as payment for your crimes."

"There is a price, however," I tell it. "You must agree to this, or I else I will not work the spell you ask, and will accept your kiss instead."

"What price?" it asks.

"It is a twofold price," I say. "First, you must allow me to inscribe a warning on the stone."

"Done," it says. "And the second?"

"You must promise that for all time, until Shalizander's final heir returns to claim the Board of the Flames from the volcano, you and your people will stay here to guard its location. And that should the Daughter of Destiny come, one of you will become her guardian in this place."

"You ask a promise of eternity, Keeper," the spirit says.

"What is eternity to you now?" I counter.

The wailing increases once more, and then the spirit says, "How shall we know the heir?"

"She will bring with her a sign of true faith," I say.

"The price is agreed. Carve your warning upon the stone and work your magic, Keeper. We will stay and guard this place, and one of us will be chosen to act as protector should Shalizander's final heir ever come here . . . with a sign of true faith."

"Agreed," I say.

Stepping around the forms, which part before me like a wispy fog, I call upon my magic and carve a warning in the stone. The first rune, the symbol of the Boards, a stylized star of Chaos—nine rays and off balance; the second rune, a symbol of fire from the Earth; the third rune, the symbol of running water; the fourth rune, the cloud-shaped symbol that means rain. It will have to be enough.

Surely, some future Keeper will know that this means to take the Board of the Flames from the bowels of the volcano will cause it to erupt once more . . . and all those in this valley to die again.

I turn back to the waiting spirits. "I will now cast the spell I promised," I say to them. "Prepare yourselves in whatever way you must, for soon, you will walk upon this Earth in the form of dogs, and your howls and barks shall serve as a warning to all who would trespass upon this sacred place."

"We are ready, Keeper," the spirit says. "Begin."

And I do.

"Remember your place, Peraud."

"My Lord?"

*"You are serving my plans, not yours. Now is not
the time for lesser conquests and mundane
pleasures."*

*"Of course, my Lord. I shall remain focused on
our goals."*

*"See that you do. Disappoint me, and you'll pay
with more than your life."*

I opened my eyes, my breath coming in sharp gasps,
filled with the two realizations of my vision.

Amber was no ordinary dog—her spirit was ancient,
and she had been chosen to protect me.

And we couldn't remove the Board of the Flames from
Vesuvius without causing another massive eruption.

Tens or even hundreds of thousands would die. How

many people lived in this area? How many children, wives, husbands, mothers, and fathers? I shuddered at the implication of the devastation that would result.

In the distance, Vesuvius rumbled like thunder, and at my feet Amber barked once, sharply, as if to say, *"See? I'll protect you, but I can't protect you from yourself."*

A wave of nausea struck me, and I felt beads of cold sweat on my forehead. Closing my eyes, I leaned my head back. I wasn't as exhausted as usual after reading the Chronicle, maybe because the vision had been less physically intense. I didn't know for sure, but the sick feeling in my stomach remained.

How could I take the Board of the Flames and doom all these people?

"That is not your concern. You must not allow yourself to quibble over human morals, Keeper," the Board of the Winds hissed. *"Our brother must be restored to us."*

"They live in the very shadow of the volcano, Keeper," the Board of the Waters added. *"They risk themselves by being here. You have no choice in your path."*

"Shut up!" I said to them. *"Just be quiet and let me think."*

Both Boards began talking at once, trying to convince me, and before I knew it, I found myself yelling aloud. "Shut up! Shut up! *Shut up!*"

The door to my room burst open, and Simon came through it, followed by Dario.

"Jenna, what's wrong?" he asked, kneeling next to the chair.

Finally, trying to calm myself over the Boards, who were now trying to soothe me as well, I remembered what Dario had taught me.

"*Vixisthra!*" I commanded them. They immediately fell silent.

"Jenna?" Dario said. "What is it? You were yelling."

I sighed wearily. *Now* I was tired. My stomach continued to do slow rolls, and all I wanted to do was curl up in bed and wait for it to pass. I didn't want to talk, didn't want to tell them. I just wanted to. . . .

"Leave me alone," I said. "Just for a little while, okay?"

"What is it?" Simon asked, with a tender concern in his voice that I'd longed to hear for days. "What's happened?"

"I don't want to talk right now, okay, Simon? Please?" I heard the desperation in my own voice and knew both men could, too.

"A burden shared is a burden halved, Jenna," Dario said, quoting the old proverb. "Let us help you."

I shook my head. "I'm all right. I just need some time to myself, okay? Please, if you want to help me, leave me alone for a while. I'm sorry I yelled, and it won't happen again. I just want to rest."

Dario nodded. "As you wish," he said. "If you need us, you know we're here for you."

Simon started to speak, but Dario reached out and grasped him firmly by the arm. "Come along, Simon," he said. "You're young enough yet that stubbornness will keep you here, when the sense of old age suggests that we do as the lady asks."

"But—" he said.

"No 'buts,'" Dario said. "We'll give her some much-needed space and rest. She'll tell us when she's ready."

"If you need us—" Simon began.

Feeling the ache in my heart, I nodded. "I'll call you," I said. "Thanks."

They left the room, shutting the battered door behind them as best they could. I got shakily to my feet and made my way to the bed, where I stretched out. Every muscle ached, and the nausea wasn't any better. Feeling the sniffles coming on, I wiped my eyes. "What do I do, Amber?" I asked the dog that was still staring intently at me, its one eye much more human than anyone else could know. "I can't kill all these people."

The dog said nothing, but her haunting stare followed me down into a sleep filled with images of fire.

When I woke up several hours later, the sun had gone down and night had claimed the villa grounds. The nausea had faded, as had some of the ache in my muscles—the ache in my heart, however, was as strong as ever. My destiny as the Keeper of the Boards was in direct conflict with my morals. My grandfather had raised me to always try to do what was right, and dooming this entire region to death was anything but that.

I took a quick shower and changed into comfortable jeans, a white tank top and a pair of sneakers. Then, with Amber following along behind, I made my way into the main dining room, following the sounds of lively conversation, music, and cutlery all mingled together.

I stopped in the arched doorway and watched as Dario clapped his hands in time to a fiddle being played and Simon made a remark to a young man seated next to him, who smiled and nodded enthusiastically.

How nice, I thought. *They're having such a good time while I'm worried sick about killing all these people to fulfill some destiny I don't even want.*

I stepped into the room, and Simon looked up and saw me. "Jenna!" he called. "Come join us!"

Dario turned his attention away from the music and extended an invitation as well, adding, "There is plenty of food and wine, young lady. Put aside your cares for tonight and relax among friends."

Several small children came forward and took my hands, leading me into the throng and to a chair across the table from Simon, next to Dario and a dark-eyed woman of perhaps fifty. She smiled at me and gestured at all the food. The table was a massive slab of oak, and it was probably groaning under the weight of all the dishes piled high in the center. I spotted several varieties of fresh-baked, rustic breads, salads with locally grown olives, at least three different types of chicken dishes in savory sauces. A large plate of cheeses, including buffalo mozzarella, caught my eye as well. My stomach rumbled, and I helped myself to a clean plate, which I began filling.

"Try the carpaccio, Jenna," Simon said, taking a bite with relish. "It's not a local dish, but they make it well." He gestured toward a plate with extremely thin slices of red meat drizzled with olive oil and capers. The plate was lined with watercress, and a dish of crackers was set next to it.

I helped myself and tried a bit. The taste was rich and exotic. "What kind of meat is this?" I asked. "It tastes like beef."

"It is," Simon said, smiling. "It's not cooked, however, which helps give it its unique flavor."

Raw meat? I thought, then shrugged. It tasted fine, and who was I to judge what other cultures liked to eat? I continued my meal while children laughed and giggled, chasing each other around the table. The middle-aged man playing the fiddle finished one song and took up another—this one a slower tune with a haunting sound that reminded me of my vision earlier in the day.

Across the table, Simon seemed in good spirits, but quiet even as the people around him laughed and talked in fluent Italian. He caught my eye several times, his gaze very direct. Finally, once I'd finished eating, he pushed his own plate aside and stood up, holding out his hand. "Will you dance with me, Jenna?"

I was so stunned by the question that for several heartbeats I didn't answer. Staring at him, I suddenly realized that he wasn't wearing the vestments of a priest, but normal clothes, although they were dark in color. Black wool slacks and a gray sweater that clung to his broad shoulders like a second skin.

I didn't say anything else, my mind racing. A small part of me felt hope spring to life, while another bled, knowing that tomorrow he'd probably be back to his old mantra about what was forbidden to a priest.

Still, a chance to dance with Simon was too much to resist, and I nodded, rising to my feet. "Yes," I said, my voice a bare whisper. "I will dance with you."

He lead me into a clear space near the violinist, and pulled me into his arms. The music was slow and steady, a waltz of some kind, and Simon moved through the steps with practiced ease while I tried not to step on his toes.

Smiling down at me, he whispered, "You haven't danced a lot in your life, have you?"

I shook my head. "Two left feet," I said.

"No," he replied, pulling me through the next steps. "Not enough practice."

Not wanting to break the spell, I couldn't help but ask a question. "How come you're not wearing your collar, your vestments?"

For a moment he didn't answer me, and I was afraid that I'd gone too far. Then he said, "Because a man who is unsure of his commitment to God shouldn't wear them."

"I . . . I don't understand," I said as the song ended on a long, sorrowful note.

Taking my hand, Simon said, "Let's go outside. I'll try to explain."

Confused, I started to follow him out onto the porch when I felt someone grasp my arm lightly. I paused and saw that Dario had walked over near the small dance floor. Leaning in, he pitched his voice so that only I could hear him. "Go easy on him, Jenna," he whispered, a gentle smile lighting his features. "In this way, he is even younger than you are, and he's obviously confused about what he should be doing."

"Tell that to my heart," I whispered back.

"I know," Dario said, "but love is *supposed* to hurt, my dear." Then he turned his attention back to a toddler who was grabbing his hand and asking for a story in a high, piping voice.

Simon led to me to the door, and as we stepped out into the night, I was determined this time to find out what he was truly thinking and feeling. We didn't speak but stood on the patio in silence for several minutes, looking up at the pinprick stars while inside the romantic music continued to play.

I wasn't sure what to say, what Simon wanted to say, so when he pulled me into his arms and began dancing slowly with me again, I kept my silence. I could feel the cool wind in my hair—a contrast to the fire his hands made where they touched mine. Slowly, he leaned down and kissed me.

I felt myself hesitate for a moment, then allowed myself to relax, kissing him back.

It was warm and wonderful, and the music playing inside, the stars all around . . . It was like a dream. He pulled away and stared into my eyes.

"I . . . I'm not quite sure what to say," I whispered. "I don't understand."

"Neither do I, Jenna," Simon said, pulling me closer. "But . . . I almost lost you, and that thought is . . . horrifying to me. It made me reconsider my feelings about a lot of different things."

"Meaning us?" I asked.

He nodded. "That's a big part of it."

"What else? This . . . it all seems so fast."

"I know," Simon said. "But ever since I met with Peraud, I've been thinking about how much of my life has been wasted time. Time spent on fear or worry, time spent trying to do the right thing even when I didn't know what it was." He looked at me directly. "I don't want to waste any more time."

I forced myself to hold on to hope, to breathe, even as I said, "Being a priest has been your whole life, Simon. I don't want to take that from you."

"One person cannot take from another what they don't want to give," he said.

"And what do you want to give?" I asked.

Without answering, he wrapped his arms more tightly around me and kissed me again. Stunned, I could almost feel the passion radiating off his body. It was heat and light, and for a few long seconds, I leaned into him, feeling like his change of heart was more than just words, but something deeper, something that was meant to happen.

Then it hit me. A feeling that was . . . wrong.

This kiss wasn't at all like the surprise kiss we'd shared in Petra, or even the gentle kiss from earlier. It almost felt like an assault on my senses.

One part of me all but screamed to give in to the passion I felt, but I'd learned that passion was an emotion that couldn't always be trusted. I didn't want to make a bad choice, as I had with Saduj, when my judgment had been less than stellar.

I pushed Simon firmly away and took a step back. "Wait a minute," I said.

"But, Jenna," he began, and I held up one hand.

"No, Simon," I said. "If this is . . . if what is between us is real, it will be there. Tomorrow and the day after and the day after that."

"I agree," he said, stepping closer. "But who knows how much time we really have? Any minute someone like Peraud could show up here and end one or both of our lives. If we don't take joy and love when we can, Jenna, we may not get to take it at all."

"I understand what you're saying, Simon," I said, fighting the urge to climb back into his arms. "But we can't. Not like this."

"Why?" he demanded, his voice suddenly stern. "What is there to stop us? Why should we stop?"

And there it was, I thought. The reason I had to stand firm. "Because, Simon, this isn't like you—like the you I've known—and if we're meant to be we will be . . . in the time we're supposed to be."

"In time?" he asked.

"Simon, I've been honest with you about how I felt, what I wanted from our relationship. But I'm not going to be a token experiment for you, while you try to figure out who you really are and what you want."

"Jenna, that's . . . that's not what I mean for you to be at all. It's just that I've realized that I couldn't have both, and that you were more important to me than my profession."

"I could never ask you to give up the priesthood, Simon," I said, taking his hand. "I don't want you to have regrets."

"I won't have regrets, Jenna," he said.

He moved toward me again, but I shook my head and stepped away. "I think you should leave me alone for right now, Simon. Go get some sleep. We'll talk more tomorrow."

"What if there is no tomorrow, Jenna?" he asked. "What if this one night is all we have?"

"Then we'll have to be content with knowing what was in our hearts," I said.

He stepped closer to me. "Let's talk more about us. Just talk."

"Us?" I asked. "Is there really an 'us'?"

"I thought that's what you wanted, Jenna," he said, his voice low and husky. "Didn't you say that kissing me was like coming home?"

Had I told him that? I couldn't remember, and his proximity was starting to affect my judgment. Then he was kissing me, and his lips were warm on mine. His hands were strong, and I felt his whole body tense as he pulled me into his embrace. One hand moved lower and lower still, and I gasped at the contact.

This was moving too fast, and *something* was out of place. My mind was racing, but if I'd learned anything since becoming the Keeper, it was to trust my instincts. I forced myself to end the kiss, to push him away.

"Let's slow down, Simon," I said. "I don't understand what you're doing and I . . . I need some time to think."

"Jenna," he said, trying to wrap me in his arms again.

I moved away again. "Simon, I'm not . . . the timing isn't right—something isn't right. I don't know what it is, but you aren't acting like yourself, and until you figure out what it is you really want in life, my heart belongs to one person—me."

I turned away from him. It was one of the hardest things I've ever had to do. "Go on now, Simon. Please." I didn't think he would, that he would keep arguing, but finally, I heard him sigh and walk away, his steps sharp staccato beats on the wooden boards of the porch. He was obviously disappointed, but I knew in my heart I'd done the right thing.

I stepped off the porch, my heart aching. If I'd stayed any longer or listened to another word, I might have crumbled. I wanted to kiss him, to have him hold me and tell me that I wasn't going to have to kill all these people. But I wanted him to do those things with his whole heart—not because he'd almost lost me or because he'd met Peraud, but because he wanted me for my own sake.

None of it made any sense.

The night air was cool, and the stars shone brightly in the dark sky. A crescent moon flickered into and out of view as clouds passed in front of it. I didn't follow any particular path, just wandered, thinking about Simon and home and how I'd ended up so far away from everything and everyone I'd ever known or dreamed of being.

The sounds of the villa faded, and I was thankful that Simon didn't follow me. I wanted to be alone and to think. Not far away, I found a small family cemetery, with all the markings of a strong Catholic faith. In the center of it, a statue of the Virgin Mary gazed down on the plots, her downcast eyes and outstretched hands a reminder that even the mother of Jesus had felt sorrow. A small white bench was situated along one of the fences, and I sat and stared up at the sky.

The bands of the Milky Way arched above me. Remembering the spirits of Pompeii, I waited and watched the headstones, but no ghosts appeared. After a few minutes, I pulled off my backpack and set it at my feet. Made of leather, it looked about as beat up as I felt. I took it everywhere with me and never let it out of my sight—it contained the four things I had to have: the two Boards, the Chronicle, and on nights like tonight, the most important thing, my BlackBerry.

I pulled it out of the pack and turned it on, wondering if the wireless Internet signal the villa advertised reached this far. It came to life, and I smiled at my luck. The signal was good. I clicked on the e-mail icon and saw that I had a message waiting for me from Tom and Kristen. Happiness flowed through through me as I opened it and read:

> Dear J.—
>
> Kristen here, checking in on you and hoping you are well.
>
> Everyone here is fine and Father Andrew sends his best wishes. You wouldn't believe it, but he's been called back to the Vatican! Some cardinal or another wants to talk with him about what happened here in Miller's Crossing. Apparently several people have called the weather phenomenon signs of the Apocalypse! Anyway, he's going to be there soon, so if you get a chance to look him up, you should.

We did some looking online about your family history, and it's very strange. We already knew that your family goes back in a straight matrilineal line—no sons at all. Your great-grandmother, Marissa, came to America when she was in her early twenties and—get this—she came on board a ship from Italy, but she wasn't Italian at all. Her citizenship was French, and she was born in Paris, according to the registry on Ellis Island. We're still doing some looking, but a lot of your family line is hard to trace because the 'Solitaire' name doesn't come up a lot, so there's not much to go on.

Other than that, we are doing well. Tom is being a good boy and keeping up with his physical therapy. He moves his wheelchair around like a pro now.

I've kept up with my "other" studies, too, and I'm sending positive energy your way. I have a new focus that Tom found for me in a shop downtown—it's an almost flawless stone that looks like a tiger's-eye, but has little jets of red in it that I'm sure are garnet. I've never had such a

wonderfully charged focus before, and I
can't imagine how a little shop in
Miller's Crossing wound up with it, but
I'm glad to have it nonetheless.

Take care of yourself, Jenna, and write
back when you can. We miss you.

Kristen

"I miss you guys, too," I whispered.

I wanted to go home. I didn't want to be the Keeper
of the Boards or the Daughter of Destiny or anything
else. I just wanted to be plain old Jenna Solitaire, struggling college student and coffee-hound about town. I
didn't want to love Simon. I didn't want to hurt anybody. I didn't want to be scared anymore.

"Feeling homesick?" a voice asked from behind me.

I turned around and saw Dario standing behind me,
one hand resting lightly on Amber's head.

"A little," I admitted, trying not to sniffle and failing
miserably.

Amber trotted forward and shoved her cold nose
into my lap. Dario sat down on the bench next to me,
moving with that uncanny grace he had of a man half
his age.

"It's a condition that you must come to terms with,
Jenna," Dario said, patting me lightly on the knee.

"Keepers don't have a home. They just have the Boards, and their goal of keeping them safe."

"Well, that just . . . sucks," I said.

And that was when I began to cry.

*"My Lord, I believe there may be a small . . .
problem."*

"Explain yourself."

*"I don't know why, but she seems very reluctant
to retrieve the Board. It is as though she knows
something we do not."*

*"Find out what the problem is, Peraud, and get
her moving. Or suffer the consequences for your lack
of persuasion."*

Dario didn't talk, just put his warm, steady arms around me and held me tight. I didn't want to cry—it seemed like that was all I did some days—but the release felt good, as did being held by someone who could have been my great-grandfather if things had worked out differently. The tears stopped almost as quickly as they'd started, and Dario offered me a handkerchief I used to wipe my eyes.

"Better?" he asked.

"Yes," I said. "Better."

"Now then," he said. "Maybe I can offer you some small comfort."

"What would that be?" I asked. "A quiet life in a nunnery somewhere?"

He laughed, and it sounded clean and good. "No, Jenna," he said. "I could never see you there. Besides, I'm afraid much of your work as Keeper of the Boards is still to come."

I sighed. "I'm afraid of that, too."

"Your great-grandmother Marissa and I spent quite some time studying the Boards and their history," he said. "The one truth to being a Keeper—even a Keeper in love—is that in many ways, you are always alone. Perhaps that's why the family name Solitaire has stuck for so long."

"I didn't want to be the Keeper of the Boards," I said. "I just wanted to go to college and live a normal life."

"Nobody *wants* the job, Jenna," he said. "Even with her other powers, Marissa didn't either. But you've got it just the same. As your mother did, and her mother and so on back into the mists of distant history. Even the Keepers who did nothing except hold the Board in some forgotten trunk—like your grandmother apparently did—could never rest easy. The Boards *call* to your family. And only your family can control them."

"Did my great-grandmother use her Board?" I asked. "Because from what I've been able to find out, no one in my family after her did."

Dario nodded. "Yes, of course," he said. "For a time she delved into their mysteries with enthusiasm. Then she stopped and went to America. I received one letter from her, a brief note saying she was sorry, and that was all."

"Did you try to stay in touch?"

"I wrote to her many times," Dario said. "I even went to America once to try and find her. I loved her very much and wanted only to understand why she did what she did."

"Did you find her?" I asked. "Did she speak to you?"

"Yes, I found her," he said, his voice a mere whisper. "But by then she was married and had given birth to your grandmother. I was too late." He shrugged. "This was all many years ago, Jenna. We never spoke again."

Saddened, I said, "I think you should have at least talked to her, found out why she'd left and stopped using the Boards."

"That much I did find out," Dario said. "Sad as it was."

I waited for him to continue, and finally he said, "The Board of the Winds got to her, I think, always talking to her and telling her to look for the Board of the Waters, promising her power and hinting at the glory awaiting her. She was a smart woman, and suspected that the

Board had its own goals in mind. Eventually she had to shut it out completely, or it would have driven her mad." He shrugged, and in the dim light he looked about two hundred years old. "At least that's what I'd like to believe."

"What do you mean?" I asked. "You mean you don't believe that?"

"Not really," he said. "Marissa was very talented, and she mastered the Board of the Winds with relative ease. She also had some magic of her own that had served her well in life."

"What kind of magic?"

"She had second-sight," he said. "She could see the future, sometimes clearly, sometimes not. I think it was her sight that caused her to stop using the Board and move to America."

"What do you think she saw?" I asked.

He smiled sadly. "I think she saw you, Jenna," he said. "And she knew that she wasn't destined to be the true Keeper of the Boards, to be the one to fulfill Shalizander's ancient prophecy."

"Oh," I said, realizing what he must think of me. "It's my fault, then, that you lost her, isn't it?"

"No, Jenna," he said, patting my knee. "You hadn't even been conceived yet! How could it have been your fault? We do not fault those whom destiny chooses for a special role. The weight of fulfilling such things is burden enough."

"You're telling me," I said, and Dario laughed. Then his face turned serious once again.

"I also believe, though I have no proof, that she may have been threatened, Jenna. Not by the Board but by someone else. Perhaps someone powerful, like this man Peraud, or even someone within the Church. The Catholic faith is in decline now, especially in America, where all the scandals have taken place recently. But back then, the Catholic faith was powerful—they created the original Templars, you know—and in Europe, they are still strong. They can be helpful allies, Jenna, but never forget that the Church has missions of its own that it will pursue. And they will have no compunction about using whomever they must to accomplish those missions. Your friend Simon is aware of this, I think."

Simon and I hadn't spoken of the Church very much, but I made a mental note to ask him about it. "Thank you, Dario," I said. "I'll remember."

"I know you will," he said. "You're very much like she was—bright, inquisitive, and very talented. Perhaps someday whatever magic flows in your veins will come forth—it just needs the right trigger, and these dreams you have are signs of it."

"I guess we'll see," I said. "But here's a question for you: What do I do about Simon?"

"What about him?" Dario asked.

"He's. . . ." My voice trailed off as I tried to describe what I felt about Simon.

"Struggling," Dario supplied. "Like many young men do."

"I could understand that," I said. "But it's like he's. . . ." I sighed, and added, "I don't know. One day, he's all business, wants to resume being a priest; then he goes and meets with Peraud and *bam*! I don't know what he's doing. What he wants. Not for sure."

"Jenna, I sense that Simon *is* a little different right now. Perhaps meeting Peraud changed his perspective. I do know that if you love him, the best you can do is be patient with him. In time, he'll figure out who he is and who he wants to be."

"Patience isn't my strong suit," I said.

"If I had a lira for every time I heard that—patience is the province of the old," Dario said, laughing. "In time, you will learn patience, too."

"I hope so," I said. I stood up and stretched, helping Dario to his feet. "It's getting late," I said, "and there's still tomorrow to deal with."

"Tomorrow will come on its own time, Jenna," Dario said. "And Simon will come around to his place in this time, too. I don't want to sound like an old man, but that's what I am. I've come to believe that God has a plan for everyone, and in time, He will reveal his plan for Simon." He patted my hand. "Simon cares for you, and deeply, Jenna. Never doubt that. When he knows his own heart, he will follow it with the same faith and confidence you've seen in him before."

"And what's in his heart?" I asked, fearing to hear an answer that wasn't what I wanted.

"Only Simon knows that," Dario said. "Love, like life, also requires a lot of patience."

We walked in silence back to the villa, with Amber trailing along behind us. My mind was racing. Tomorrow, I would have to face the truth of my vision. To take the Board of the Flames would doom all of these people to death.

If that was what it meant to be the Keeper of the Boards, then I couldn't do it. That much of my heart I knew for sure.

I didn't see Simon when I walked through the villa and escorted Dario to his room, but not long after I closed the door to my room and shoved a chair beneath the knob to hold it in place, he knocked on the polished wood.

"Jenna?" he called. "Are you still awake?"

"What is it, Simon?" I asked, not bothering to get out

of bed. "I'm tired and want to get some sleep."

"Can we talk for a minute?" he asked. "Please?"

I sighed. "I think I'm about talked out for today, Simon. We can talk tomorrow."

He stirred on the other side of the door, but must have decided not to push. "Okay," he said. "I just want to apologize for my earlier behavior. I shouldn't have pushed you. We've got plenty of time to figure things out between us."

Thinking of Dario's words earlier, I said, "Your apology is accepted, Simon. We all make mistakes now and then."

"Good," he said. "May I come in for a minute, then?"

I was about to say yes when I noticed Amber. She was sitting in front of the door, staring at it. Low in her throat, I heard a soft growl. She had avoided Simon from the minute he'd shown up during my fight with the spirits in Pompeii, and I suspected that if I opened the door, she'd probably bite him.

"Not tonight, Simon," I said. "We'll talk more tomorrow, okay?"

"Okay, Jenna," he said. "Good night."

"Good night, Simon," I said.

I watched Amber, but she remained poised by the door for several minutes before finally lowering her head. Turning down the lamp next to the bed, I curled up beneath the covers with the BlackBerry and wrote an e-mail back to Tom and Kristen.

Dear T&K—

Thanks for sending me the note about my family and Father Andrew. We're supposed to be going back to Rome when we're done here, so if there's a chance, I'll definitely try to find him and say hello.

Things here are good and bad. Dario is helping me find ways to deal with the Boards, but Simon is. . . . <sigh> I don't know. Trying to find himself, I guess. Speaking of weird relations, it turns out that he and Peraud are brothers, identical twins, and they met recently. Simon came back from that meeting with a lot on his mind, and I think he's very confused.

I've also inherited a new friend. Pompeii is filled with stray dogs—someday I'll tell you why—and one of them, a German shepherd I've named Amber, has practically become my shadow. She's a good guard dog and quiet, so it's nice to have her around.

There's something I'm hoping you can find out for me. After my great-grandmother came to America, where did she go? Did she come to Ohio right away? I've got a hunch that she didn't, and maybe we can find someone else besides Dario who knew her. It's a long shot, but it's worth a try.

Oh, something else, too. Can you check out the history of Mount Vesuvius? Anything on the times it has erupted and what the damage was to the surrounding area.

Give Father Andrew my e-mail address and the BlackBerry number and have him send me his contact info in Rome so I can find him when I get there. Glad to hear you've got a new focus stone, whatever that is, exactly—just be careful with things like that. Magic of any kind, as we both know, can be dangerous.

Take care of yourselves!

All my love,

Jenna

I shut down the BlackBerry and clicked off the lamp next to the bed. As I drifted down into sleep, I heard Amber's low growl again and I sat up, but she appeared to be sleeping. I lay back down and closed my eyes, thinking about tomorrow and having to tell Simon and Dario that I couldn't do it. I couldn't take the Board of the Flames and kill all these people.

If following my heart meant that Peraud or someone would get the Board first, then so be it. At least there wouldn't be any more blood on my hands.

And that was the image I took into my sleep and deeper, into my dreams. Blood on my hands.

The Tower is going to fall. Not today or tomorrow, but soon. It groans beneath the weight of the ages, the bricks cracking with the strain of holding in all those secret magics. When it falls, it will level the countryside for miles around. I look out a window at the city below.

The hanging gardens and secret mazes will be gone.

The people dead or hiding, taking refuge with one of the other lost tribes wandering the desert in search of salvation or faith.

The city empty and desolate, lost beneath the red sands of the desert that claim all things in time.

I climb the steps to my mother's room and knock on her door. Her servant lets me in, leaving the room and shutting the door behind us.

It is time and past time. And still I hesitate.

In her small bed, my mother's body looks ravaged by the ages. She has lived many years, worked magics great and small. Her hands helped guide the creation of the Boards of Chaos, and it was her magic that held them in check. And now those magics are devouring her alive. Standing in the threshold to her room, I stare at the woman I have known so long and cannot bring myself to help.

"Malizander," she says. Her voice is the whisper of a ghost, a dried reed bough rubbing on rock.

"Mother," I say, crossing the room to sit next to her bed. The window has been left open, and a breeze comes in, scented with desert secrets. "You look well."

"You should not lie, Malizander," she says. "It's not your best skill."

I smile, and her eyes, once as bright as cut emeralds, now faded and cloudy, lock with mine. "I know," I tell her.

"It is time, Malizander," she whispers. "You must do this last thing for me."

"Mother," I start to say, but she holds up a hand, wrinkled and spotted, to forestall my words.

"You must do this for me, Malizander," she repeats. "The magic of the Boards is too much for me, they . . . consume me. You must take the mantle of the Keeper."

"I don't want it," I whisper. "You are the Keeper of the Boards, not I."

"Foolish child," she snaps with a hint of her old power.

"My time is long past. You know the prophecy. You must take the Boards and hide them as I've instructed you. In time, they will sleep."

"They'll be my death," I say. "I do not have your strength."

"You do, child," she says. "You have but to use it."

She leans back into her pillows, her outburst tiring her. I know I must do as she asks, as she has asked me every day for the last weeks. But knowing is not the same as willing.

"Mother," I say, leaning down close to her. "Do not ask this of me. There must be another way."

Her eyes fix on mine, and with a hand palsied by age, she strokes my hair. "My child," she says. "Would that this burden had never been passed to us, but it has. We must stop Malkander, and the only way to do that is to hide the Boards from him. You must take my role as the Keeper. In time, he will die, and our heirs will continue doing as we have done."

"Will he?" I ask, doubtful. My mother had been a great sorceress, but Malkander . . . his power is seemingly without limits.

"All things die," she says. "In time." She coughs once and then gasps to catch her breath. "And my time is now, Malizander."

I shake my head, unwilling to accept it, but I know she is right. There is no point in delaying, no reason to do so. Her orders have been followed, and a ship stands ready to carry me wherever I desire. A caravan waits in the square below, should I choose to travel by land. The Boards are packed into a chest in my room, and their multitude of voices already clamor for my attention.

All that remains is this final task.

"Please, Malizander," my mother whispers. "There is no other choice."

I stand and walk numbly to the window that looks out over Babylon. This is a city of the dead, and they don't even know it yet. The citizens go about their lives as always, not burdened with my mother's visions. Or mine. The wind blows soft on my face, and I reach my decision.

Moving with care, I cross to my mother's worktable. Years of rituals have scarred its surface, and dark stains mark the smooth wood. Stains of fire and of blood.

In the center of the worktable is my mother's last magical creation. A dagger with a wavy edge and a wicked point. The metal is whorled and soaks up any light that strikes it. She has told me that the blade was heated and folded over a thousand times. The blade itself is imbued with magics, and when I lift it from the table, it trembles in my hand, hungry for blood.

This blade feeds on life and magic, its sole purpose the destruction of mages. Her destruction.

I don't turn around as I grasp the hilt in my fist. "Are you sure?" I ask.

"Yes, child," she says. *"You have the strength and know what you must do."*

She has told me that this blade will penetrate the magical shields that protect her body from physical harm. That it will shatter them like so much glass and then. . . .

"It will release me," she says. *"And, if you have the strength, it will save you."*

I do not know if I have the strength. If I am brave enough. If my hand will stop shaking long enough to do what she asks.

"I love you, Mother," I say. I fix her image in my mind—not the withered husk she has become, but the beautiful woman she once was. The magic did this to her, and now I will undo it.

"I love you, too, child," she says. *"Now strike, before fears claims you!"*

I do not hesitate or let another word stay my hand. I turn and in three quick strides cross to her bed, the dagger held high over my head.

It catches the light of the sun sinking into the west and shining into the window.

It screams as it arcs downward, propelled by my hand.

It plunges through her shields, which burst around the blade in a shower of sparks.

And then it is in her heart.

It twitches in my hands, drinking her life and her magic in great, heaving gulps.

The hilt grows hot, and I open my eyes to look once more at my mother's face. She is dying and does not speak. In a minute, it is done. Her magics and her spirit are gone, now held inside the blade. I remove it from her chest, and a small spatter of blood, wet and red, flicks off the blade and onto my hands.

The shell of her body is empty and useless now, and I ignore it as I lie down in the bed next to her.

I am afraid. Her mind and magics were strong until the end, but what if she is wrong? What if this won't work?

Time is running out. She said it had to be quick.

I hold the dagger in both hands. I lift it over my heart.

My heart races, beating against the frame of my chest like a rabbit in a trap.

"Strike, Malizander!" I hear my mother's voice say. "Strike now and save us all!"

I plunge the blade into my chest, and the magic courses through me.

I am Malizander.

I am Shalizander.

I am the dagger.

I am all three and more.

I rise from the bed, and pluck the dagger from my chest. Blood spatters once more, but the magics quickly heal the wound.

"You have done well, child," my mother says inside my mind. "Now there is hope."

"I am the Keeper of the Boards," I tell her. "Where must I—we—go?"

"Into the desert, child," she says. "To hide the Board of the Waters."

I leave her rooms and make my way to the waiting caravan. The journey will be long, but at least I will not be lonely.

"My Lord, it will soon be done. The Keeper and all three Boards will be in my grasp."

"And then you will return her and the Boards to me. Do not fail in this, Peraud. With the Keeper and the first three Boards in hand, we will soon uncover the hiding place of the last Board of the Elements. Finish it."

I woke the next morning with my mind whirling. There was so much to consider, including what I had learned in my dream the night before. Where was the dagger that contained Shalizander's soul? If it still existed, could I harness its magics for myself? Would it somehow help me in my role as the last Keeper?

Still, there were other issues that needed to be solved—like if taking the Board of the Flames out of Vesuvius was even the right decision to begin with—

and I felt uncomfortable discussing them with Simon. My grandfather had once told me that people in the middle of an identity crisis couldn't be trusted to make wise decisions, and experience had proven him right.

I pulled out my BlackBerry and dialed the number for Armand.

He answered on the second ring. "Jenna?" he said. "What's wrong?"

Putting aside my discomfort of having people answer the phone with my name instead of a polite hello, I said, "Nothing, really. I just need to know something."

"What's that?" he asked.

"Do I have to secure the Boards in any particular order?"

"I . . . I believe so," he said. "Is there a problem trying to retrieve the Board of the Flames?"

"Yes," I said. I described the warning left by Malizander, and heard Armand's stiff gasp when I told him that Vesuvius would erupt again if the Board was removed.

"Are you absolutely certain, Jenna?" he asked when I finished.

"I'm pretty sure," I said. "A lot of people would die, Armand."

"I understand," he said. There was a long moment of silence on the line. Then he continued, "Jenna, what we're doing . . . it's more important than the lives we're talking about. I know that sounds harsh, but it is also the truth. If Peraud or someone like him gets hold of the Boards, the world will become a much darker place."

"Where do we draw the line, Armand?" I asked. "When do we become like those we despise?"

"It's a difficult problem, Jenna, and there is no easy answer," he admitted. "But what will life for those people—and people everywhere—be like if Peraud secures the Board first? Will it be death, or something worse than death?"

I didn't answer him, and Armand pushed his point home. "Jenna, what we're doing is much more than collecting magical trinkets. Being the Keeper of the Boards means making life-and-death decisions, and sometimes those decisions affect many other people, in ways you wouldn't have thought possible. You must secure the Board of the Flames—or someone else, someone worse—will."

"You mean like Peraud," I said.

"Yes, like Peraud," Armand said.

"Did Simon tell you he met with him? That they think they're identical twins?" I asked.

The silence that greeted this question was answer enough. "He didn't, did he?"

"No," Armand admitted. "He . . . hasn't been in touch with me in the past couple of days. Do you know what was said?"

"Not really. But Simon stopped wearing the vestments of a priest, and he's . . . I don't know. He says he's trying to find himself."

"Hmmm. . . ." Armand's voice trailed off in thought. "Jenna, how have things worked out with Dario? Has he been able to help you?"

Trying to figure out the change of subject, I said, "Yes, yes he has. He's been wonderful. Why?"

"I want you to do something for me," Armand said. "I want you to ask Dario to keep an eye on Simon."

"What do you mean?"

"Dario was once a priest, and he's very wise," Armand said. "It may be that his experiences will serve you well in guiding Simon through this difficult period. Just speak with him about it, if you would."

"Okay," I said.

"Dario has served the cause of the Templars for a long time. Perhaps he will sense if something is truly amiss with Simon." He paused, then continued, "Jenna, you need to retrieve the Board of the Flames and then return to Rome. I have a sense that things are moving even more quickly now, coming to a head, though it may be nothing more than my imagination, to be honest."

"I'll see what I can do, Armand," I said. "But to tell you the truth, I'm not comfortable with any of this. I won't kill all these people. There's enough blood on my hands already." The words brought my dream from the night before back to me, and I shuddered at the thought of what Malizander had done.

"I know, Jenna," he said. "But in the end, you'll see that you're doing the right thing. Now, is there anything else I can do for you?"

"One thing," I said. "Have you ever heard of a special dagger that Shalizander made and that was carried by her daughter? A magical dagger."

"Not offhand," Armand said. "Why?"

"I had a dream about it," I said. "If we could find that dagger. . . ."

"Yes?" Armand prompted.

"I think it would be a big help to us," I finished. "Just see what you can find out about it, okay?"

"Certainly, Jenna," he said. "Stay in touch, and be sure to talk to Dario."

"I will, Armand," I said. "Good-bye."

I shut down the BlackBerry, then stuffed it in my backpack alongside the Boards and the Chronicle. Then I headed downstairs to find coffee and breakfast and to break the bad news to Simon and Dario.

No matter what I'd said to Armand, I couldn't go through with it. If Peraud or some other evil sorcerer wanted the Board of the Flames, the blood of the innocent people living in this region would be on their hands, not mine.

There are simply some rules I couldn't bring myself to break. My unwillingness to massacre thousands of innocents was certainly one of them.

"What do you mean you're aren't going to get it?" Simon asked, dismay written across his face. "We have to!"

"No, we don't," I said. "*We* don't have to do anything. And neither do I."

Setting down his coffee, Simon steepled his fingers, almost as if he were praying to me. "Jenna, you need to think about what you're saying," he said. "The Board of the Flames *must* be calling to you by now. Do you want someone like . . . like Peraud used to be to get it first?"

"If the Board of the Flames is removed from Mount Vesuvius, it will erupt," I said. "End of story. I won't be responsible for that many deaths, Simon. I won't."

"How do you know that?" he asked. "You're making an assumption based on a vision? What if the Chronicle is wrong? What if Malizander was wrong or she lied?"

"So far, everything I've learned from the Chronicle has been right on, Simon," I said. "I won't take that chance."

Dario sat quietly, sipping his coffee, his head cocked to one side or another as we sparred.

"You're being ridiculous," Simon snapped.

"No, she's not," Dario said, his voice clear and calm. "She's being true to her values. Something I think you would usually appreciate about her."

"I do!" Simon protested, then lowered his voice. "This isn't a game we're playing, Dario. Finding the Boards and keeping them away from people who would do evil is more important than just about anything in the world."

Dario shook his head. "Simon, you're young yet, and impetuous. And you haven't learned to compromise worth a damn." He took a sip of his coffee. "You *and* Jenna both need to learn a little something about that, I think."

"So what's the compromise?" I asked.

"Examine the situation," Dario said. "Long ago, I journeyed up Vesuvius and found a very old trail that leads deep into the volcano. I can take you there. If you can find the Board, maybe look at how it's protected, perhaps you can find a way to get it *and* keep Vesuvius from erupting. The worst you've lost is some time. If you walk away now, however, you won't have gained anything."

Simon sat back, a self-satisfied grin on his face.

Dario ignored Simon's expression and continued. "Of course, if you find that you don't like the situation or can't figure out a way to get the Board out, then I support your decision fully, Jenna," he said. "I would, I think, like you a lot less if you were willing to kill that many people to achieve your goals."

Simon's grin faded a little, and I nodded. Dario's plan made sense. Perhaps some other clues remained where the Board was located that would allow me to safely remove it.

"Agreed," I said. "Let's finish our breakfast and get going. I have a feeling it's going to be a long day."

Outside, the volcano rumbled as if already complaining about our plan, and Simon gulped down the last of his coffee. "I'll go make arrangements for transportation to the base of the volcano," he said, getting out of his seat. Suddenly he seemed filled with nervous energy. "I'll meet the two of you outside in a few minutes."

He left, and Dario and I finished our breakfast in companionable silence. As we rose to leave, Dario grasped my arm. "Are you all right, Jenna?" he asked. "You seem . . . upset."

"It's nothing, really," I said. "But I would like to ask a favor of you, if I may."

"Anything at all," Dario replied, smiling.

"Can you . . . keep an eye—"

"On Simon," he finished. "I already have been. And I will continue to do so."

"You have?" I asked. "Why?"

"Because a crisis of identity is difficult on anyone," Dario said. "But on a priest, it is especially challenging. The demands of the faith are many, the rewards few. I don't know if or how Simon can reconcile his very human desires with his faithful ones, but I do pray that he can figure it out quickly. I don't like seeing him this way."

I smiled grimly. "Neither do I."

We went out into the morning sunlight, Amber on our heels, and began the journey to Vesuvius. Beneath our feet, the ground trembled some more, and in the distance, a long, thin plume of smoke rose from the peak of the volcano. I wondered briefly if the Board of the Flames knew I was here, and the Board of the Waters answered in my mind.

"Our brother has never slept, Keeper. Not in all these centuries. He has been waiting for you for a long time."

"You mean he doesn't have to be awakened?" I asked.

"Yes, Keeper," the Board replied. *"That is why the volcano keeps erupting. He uses his abilities for his own amusement. Fire is his plaything, much as water is mine."*

"So will it erupt if I take the Board from here?" I asked.

"Should my brother desire it, Keeper, the entire moun-

tain will explode in an eruption the likes of which has never been seen before."

"*That's just about perfect,*" I said.

I climbed into the old truck that Simon had rented from the villa, and Amber jumped into the back. The important part of our time here, I realized, was about to begin.

Overhead, the smoke rising into the sky from the top of Vesuvius took on different shapes. It wasn't lost on my imagination that all of the shapes appeared to look like flames.

From a distance, the greenery that crawled up the side of Mount Vesuvius looked picturesque. Up close, it looked a lot more like thorns. A lot of long, sharp thorns. We'd driven to the base of the volcano while Dario recited landmarks from memory like he was reading a map.

"How do you do that?" I asked him.

"Do what?"

"Remember details so well?"

He smiled. "As you get older, Jenna, you may find that your memory is all that is left of the life you once lived. The pictures in my mind make up, in some small way perhaps, for having lived so long that all my friends and loved ones are gone." He paused, then added, "When you get to the place in the road where three boulders sit atop each other, stop. We should be close."

Sure enough, Simon guided the old truck around a curve, and the three boulders, resting on top of each other as if stacked by a giant hand long ago, appeared. "We're here," he said, pulling off the road.

"Very good," Dario said as we climbed out. "Now the real test of my memory begins."

"How so?" I asked.

"There are many footpaths that traverse this area," he replied. "If I choose the wrong one, we won't reach our destination, but just wander around on the mountain aimlessly."

"Let's just get going," Simon said. "The sooner we can take a look at where the Board is, the faster we can figure out how to get it out of here without destroying the surrounding countryside."

"*If* we can," I mumbled.

"Which way?" Simon asked Dario.

"Go around the boulders," Dario replied. "There should be a small footpath leading up."

His memory guiding us, Dario led us slowly up the side of the volcano. Amber ambled along behind us, stopping from time to time to sniff the air; and once, when the earth shuddered violently beneath us, she barked as if in warning.

All of us stopped and looked up, expecting to see an eruption, but other than the previous cloud of smoke, nothing new appeared. The ground around us, however, was a different story. Steam seeped out of cracks in the earth, escaping with a hissing sound that reminded me more than a little of the voice of the Board of the Winds. The ground rolled again, and more steam vents opened higher up.

"This could get ugly in a hurry," I said, watching Amber eye the terrain ahead with stiff-backed caution, her tail tucked between her legs.

"And dangerous," Simon said. "So let's hurry right along."

We kept moving as the ground shuddered beneath our feet. Several times, rocks and other debris rolled past as we followed Dario's hurried instructions. I didn't know if we were going in the right direction or not, but our course continued upward, and I had no choice but to trust his memory.

After more than an hour of steady climbing, all of us were sweating and exhausted. A rocky overhang offered some shelter, and I leaned against a boulder and said, "Let's take a break. I'm beat."

Simon and Dario agreed and found seats for themselves nearby. All of us drank heavily from water bottles Dario had had the foresight to bring along, and I poured some in my cupped hand for Amber to lap at. We rested for several minutes, and I was just about to get to my feet when a violent shudder rocked the ground beneath us. It felt like an earthquake, and I jumped up and out of the way just as the rocky overhang I had been under collapsed.

"Are you all right, Jenna?" Dario asked.

"Just scared out of my wits; otherwise, I'm great, thanks," I replied.

"Look up there," Simon said, pointing. "That *can't* be good,"

Perhaps three hundred feet above us, a large shelf of rock tilted at a sharp angle. The ground continued to roll, and with a loud crack, the shelf broke loose. Amber barked once and began to move away, but in those long, slow seconds, I knew there was nowhere to run.

"Get close to me!" I yelled. "Amber, come!"

Simon and Dario crowded close, and Amber loped forward to sit at my feet.

"I am the Keeper of the Boards. Your will is my will. Answer my call!" My mental summons flashed out, even as high above, the rock shelf slammed into the ground with terrific force and began sliding toward us.

The Board of the Winds replied in its hissing voice. *"What is your will, Keeper?"*

"I need a cyclone to levitate us over this rockslide—NOW!"

Jolted into action, the Board's power flared, and the winds stirred around us in a circle, whirling and spinning like a top. I looked up and knew we weren't going to make it. The rockslide was nearly halfway to us and picking up speed. Small rocks showered down on us.

"Faster!" I demanded.

The Board didn't reply, but I felt another surge in the magic, and the winds suddenly swirled with raging force. I reached out with my mind, trying to bend the winds to my will. I wanted them to encircle us, lift us up, but other than one time by accident, I'd never tried to do this.

It was like trying to lift those boulders at the bottom of the trail.

"Jenna, hurry!" Simon said. "It's almost on us!"

"Now!" I commanded the Board.

The Board flared out once more, and the winds began to lift us up just as the leading edge of the rockslide slammed into the ground where we'd been standing. I heard Dario yell in pain, but I ignored him, forcing myself to continue calling on the cyclone that lifted us over the barrage of rocks cascading down the mountainside. When the roar of their passing stopped, I slowly relaxed my will.

"Lower us, gently," I commanded the Board.

"As you will, Keeper," it replied.

The winds slowed, and we began to descend back to the earth. The trail we had been following was gone. The thorny shrubs that had littered the mountainside had been uprooted by the rolling rocks. It now looked like the barren landscape of the moon.

We settled back to the ground and Dario immediately yelped in pain and collapsed. Amber barked several times, looking around with her tail between her legs.

"Remarkable, Jenna," Simon said, scanning the altered landscape. "Your control is most impressive."

I ignored his odd comment and went to Dario, who was holding his left leg off the ground and muttering in Italian. "What's wrong?" I asked.

"A rock slammed into my leg just as you lifted us," he said between gritted teeth. "I'm afraid that it's broken."

I knelt at his feet and gingerly rolled up the pant leg. A large bruise was already forming on the front of his shin, which was dimpled from the impact. "I'd say so," I said. "Simon, come take a look at this."

He didn't reply, and I turned around to say something to him when I noticed the direction of his stare. Above us, where the shelf had come loose, an entrance into the side of the volcano was clearly visible. It wasn't a natural opening, but rather had been carved from the rock by some terrific force, the sides squared off in perfect angles. Above it, carved into the stone, was the nine-rayed Star of Chaos.

"Look at that," I whispered. "If only they were all so clearly marked."

"The rockslide must have exposed it," Simon said. "I thought we must have been getting close. Why didn't you say anything, Dario?"

"This isn't the time for criticism, Simon," I said, getting to my feet to stand beside him. "He's got a broken leg."

"Actually," he said, "this is a perfect time for criticism. His journey is about to end."

"What are you talking about now?" I asked.

He whistled sharply, the sound echoing over the landscape so loudly that I knew it wasn't a natural whistle, but enhanced somehow. Amber's ears went back against her head, and a low growl rumbled in her throat.

Above us, a large group of nearly a dozen men come out of the rocks, several of them battered from the rockslide, but all of them able and armed to the teeth. Leading them was an all-too-familiar figure.

My shoulders sagged.

The man would *never* give up. Not for blood or money.

His coin was magic and power. And he would pay whatever price he needed to in order to claim me and the Boards.

What was more terrible was that Simon had apparently included himself in that purchase, leading us directly to his brother . . . Peraud.

"Our plan is revealed, my Lord, in all its cold wonders."

"And the Keeper?"

"As you predicted long ago. Her heart leads her to make decisions that weaken her and make her vulnerable to manipulation."

"Excellent. See that this opportunity is not wasted."

There are moments in life when time slows down, seconds passing us in frame-by-frame motion. Car accidents. An attacking dog. The death of a loved one.

Betrayal.

Looking at Simon, the satisfied smile on his face, the only thing I could think of was that his need for a family had been more troubling to him than I had imagined. As small as it was, I had at least *had* a family.

Simon was an orphan, and the lack of a family must have haunted him for years. Somehow, some way, Peraud had convinced him to change sides. To betray me and everything we'd worked for.

From above, Peraud said, "All right, we're all here." His voice sounded tired and weary, and with the sun behind him, I couldn't see his face. "Let's finish this."

Simon nodded and turned back to me and Dario. "Your assistance has been quite useful, old man, but your time on this Earth is done."

Dario gritted his teeth and looked up at Simon. "There is a darkness waiting for you that will make my death seem like the light of a new day."

Without another word, his face red with anger, Simon whipped a dagger out from beneath his shirt, and before I could do more than draw a breath to scream, he knelt and slashed Dario's throat.

The world went silent for several seconds as a thin, red line appeared just below Dario's larynx, crossing to either side like a red smile. He tilted his head to one side, as though he were listening for something only he could hear; then it tilted completely over, and the blood flowed freely to soak into the dusty rock.

Ignoring Simon, Peraud, everyone and everything, I rushed to where Dario lay on the rocky ground. I heard his breath whistling out of the wound in his throat. I sobbed, knowing that even with all of the so-called power at my command, there was nothing I could do. Nothing anyone could do.

"Dario," I whispered, bending down close to his ear. "I'm so sorry."

Still trying to breathe through the wound, his voice gurgled, the sound wet and fading. "Don't . . . don't. . . ." He struggled with the words.

"Shhh," I said. "Just rest now." My hands were slick with his blood, and for a moment, I thought of the dream, of the dagger. Of Peraud, who had corrupted even Simon.

He gasped and clutched at me with his hands. "Don't . . . believe . . . everything you . . . see!" he said.

"What do you mean?" I asked. "I don't understand."

"Ahhh . . . Marissa," he whispered. "I should have . . . told her."

And then he was gone.

I sat there with Dario's head cradled in my lap for a full minute, perhaps longer, before I became aware of Amber. She sat nearby, staring at me and howling at the top of her lungs. I ignored her. My guardian or not, she should have protected Dario, too.

I eased his head off my lap and down to the ground, shutting his eyelids gently. Then I stood and turned to face Simon. The man I had known could never have done such a horrible thing, such an evil thing. It was like he was suddenly someone else or possessed by some dark demon. It was impossible, yet the truth of it was dead on the ground at my feet.

I tried to find words, some way to express my shock, and could only stutter incoherently. He was no longer my friend, no longer a priest. He wasn't anything except someone who had killed an innocent old man whom I had loved and respected. And he did it for no reason.

Trembling with rage, I took a step forward. "You . . . I don't even *know* you . . . you sick freak!"

Simon wiped the keen edge of the blade on the old man's shirt and replaced it in the sheath. The coin necklace he wore winked in the sun. He saw my stare and grinned. "Oh, come now, Jenna," he said. "He was a feeble old man. He'd outlived his usefulness. You should be thankful that I've put him out of his misery."

From above, Peraud called out, "That's enough! Leave her alone!"

Surprised, I turned and saw one of the men shove him hard from behind. Peraud stumbled forward and fell to his knees. That's when the sun disappeared behind a bank of clouds and I saw him clearly for the first time.

His face was bruised, and his hands were bound behind his back. He wore the black vestments of a priest, the white collar loose and flapping around his neck. And his eyes, desperate and dark, caught mine.

The man who'd killed Dario *wasn't* Simon, he was Peraud!

Stunned by this revelation, that I hadn't seen it sooner, I tottered back several steps, tripped over a rock, and landed on my butt next to Amber. How could I not have seen it? He hadn't even really tried to act like Simon, and I had been too foolish and blind to see the difference!

"Ah, I see you've finally figured it out," Peraud said. "I *was* beginning to wonder about your powers of observation, Jenna." He took a step forward, and Amber bounded between us, teeth bared and growling low in her throat.

"Of course," he added, "what I'd really hoped was that you would let me into your room the other night so we could ... make up for our little spat." He grinned and pointed at the dog. "Your little guardian there convinced you otherwise. I think it's about time for her to return to her own plane of existence, don't you?"

As he raised his hands to cast some sort of spell, I yelled, "Don't!"

Quirking an eyebrow, he asked, "Why? Having that creature around isn't going to help you or Simon."

"I know you're planning on killing us anyway," I said, thinking quickly. "But for all that she's a guardian, she's still only a dog. Why waste your power killing her? You may need it to deal with me, remember? I'll send her away."

"**Then do so**," Peraud snapped. "And quickly."

I got back to my feet, and brushed myself off. "Amber, go," I said. "Get out of here."

She cocked her head at me, her golden eye fixed on me as if to say, *"Are you crazy, lady? That's a very bad man over there."*

"I know," I told her. "Go on. Get!"

She barked once, then turned and loped down the mountainside. I was sorry to see her go. I'd grown used to her quiet, comforting presence.

I looked at Peraud. "There, are you happy now?"

"No," he said. "But I will be when you hand over your backpack."

"What if I just called on their powers?" I asked. "And blew you right off the side of this mountain?"

Peraud laughed. "You won't, Jenna. Because if I feel so much as a twitch of magical energy, I won't hesitate to have my men put a bullet in the back of Simon's head." He looked up to where one of his men had dragged Simon to his feet, a pistol near his head. "He's had a very difficult few days. Death might feel like a blessing to him, too."

"All right—all right!" I said. I pulled the pack off my shoulders and handed it over to him. "You win."

"That's much better. Now," he said, slipping one of the straps over his arm, "we'll go on up, and as a group, we'll all go after the Board of the Flames. *You* will retrieve it for me, and there will be no room for error, Jenna. I'll kill Simon if you so much as look at me funny. Do we understand each other?"

"Clear as crystal," I said. "Let's just get this over with. I'd rather be dead than spend another minute longer than I have to in your presence."

"Such a charmer," he said. He gestured up the rocky incline. "After you, Keeper."

I started up what was left of the path while Peraud's men waited for us. Once there, I stopped and got a good look at Simon. They'd knocked him around quite a bit, but more than anything else, he looked angry. His eyes were the same color as they had been when he'd punched out an antiquities dealer named Burke who'd tried to kidnap me back in Miller's Crossing.

"I'm sorry," he said. "I should have listened to you. I . . . I know better than to trust someone like that."

I shook my head. "No, Simon, I'm the one who's sorry. I should have known that slug wasn't you." I put my arms around him and kissed him on the cheek. "I know all too well what it's like to want a family, to want to hold onto them with both hands and never let go."

"Enough with the touching reunion," Peraud said. He grabbed the back of my shirt and pulled backward. "Let's get moving."

We began working our way to the tunnel entrance, and a thought occurred to me. "So, Peraud, how are you going to get out of here once I've gotten the Board for you? You know this place is going to go up like a rocket."

He smiled. "I don't intend to be here for the fireworks," he said, sounding confident. "You and Simon, however, will be on your own. Then you'll find out how good you are without the Boards to help you."

"Why didn't you just kidnap Simon and demand my help?" I asked. "Seems like it would've been easier than posing as him and going through all the rigmarole of getting here."

"Now that's very astute of you." He paused, then shrugged as though reaching a decision. "Unlike my brother, I'm not dealing with a crisis of conscience. I found you attractive and thought that getting to know you better would be desirable. Seeing you believe, if only for a second, that Simon had betrayed you was purely a bonus."

"Ugh," I said. "I'd rather be dead than have you touch me again."

"I tasted the fire on your lips last night, Keeper, when you believed I was your precious Simon. It's obvious that you're in love with him. I could feel it in every pathetic beat of your frightened heart."

I heard Simon's sharp intake of breath behind me and ignored it. "It doesn't matter, does it?" I asked. "He's a priest, and that's the end of it. I won't hurt him that way."

"If only love were so noble," he retorted. "But love is of the flesh as much as the heart. The flesh is weak, Jenna. If the two of you had more time—and you don't—he'd see the errors of his ways and make a woman out of you."

Seething, I said, "Something *you* couldn't do on your best day with a multivitamin, Wheaties, and a handful of Viagra."

Without missing a beat, Peraud's hand shot out and slapped me. "I've had enough of your mouth to last a lifetime, *Keeper*. Shut up and lead the way."

My cheek stung, but inside I felt triumphant. Finally, a tiny crack in the armor. It had been worth it just to see the startled anger on his face. Peraud obviously preferred his women silent and submissive.

"As soon as I have the third Board in my possession, I'll be on my way to retrieve the fourth Board, and the key that will allow me to become master of the elements," Peraud said. "Until then, keep your mouth shut and do as I say."

I wondered how he planned on doing that, since only someone born of Shalizander could fully control the Boards, but I didn't dare ask. If he had a methodology of using the Boards, I was pretty sure I didn't want to know.

"And who is your master, Peraud?" Simon asked from behind us.

"What do you mean?" the sorcerer asked, feigning innocence and doing it badly.

"Every dog has a leash, Peraud," Simon said. "And the bigger the dog, the stronger the leash. Who holds yours?"

Peraud stiffened and stopped walking, turning to stare back at his twin. "I may have a leash, brother, but I guarantee it's more flexible than that chafing collar you wear. Don't push me any further. There are lines I'll cross without hesitation that would give you nightmares for the rest of your life."

Simon didn't say anything else.

Peraud turned back to me and said, "Get moving!"

I followed the best available path higher, my mind running in frantic circles. How could I stop Peraud from getting away with the Boards, let alone from killing everyone around here—myself and Simon included—when I took the Board of the Flames?

I shot a mental query at the Board of the Winds. *"Do you have any ideas?"*

"Keeper, each Board must be mastered. We are not the toys of children, easily taken up or put aside."

"What do you mean?" I asked.

"What my brother is saying," the Board of the Waters interrupted, "is that each of us is unique. The challenge of mastering us varies, dependent not on the Keeper as much as on our will. I chose to not fight you for control when you discovered me in Petra. My brother, the Board of the Flames, will."

"Why? Isn't having me as Keeper in his best interest to 'open the way,' whatever that means?"

The Board of the Winds responded, "Perhaps, but my brother relishes his freedom, and will not submit easily. Also, Peraud is more than capable of lying about his intentions. It would be a mistake to kill you out of hand. He would then have to wait for many years before he could attempt to awaken us once more and master our powers."

"So you don't think Peraud will really try to kill me?"

The Board of the Waters laughed. "It wouldn't be the intelligent course of action, Keeper. He would do better to try and turn you into an ally, or at least continue to use your abilities until he achieves his goals."

I thought about what the Boards were saying, and it made a great deal of sense. Peraud needed me, at least until he could master the Boards—which wasn't really possible because. . . . "He can't be the Keeper of the Boards!"

"*Very good, Keeper,*" the Board of the Winds said. "*He cannot master us. He can use our powers to some extent, but we would never bow to his will like we do for you. He is not of Shalizander's line.*"

"*Which means I'm safer than he wants me to believe I am.*"

"*A reasonable deduction, Keeper. Peraud knows that should you fall, we will no longer be bound by the covenant of magic wrought by Shalizander and Malkander. We will bow to no one, not even Peraud's master.*"

"*Who is Peraud's master?*" I asked.

Ahead, I saw the opening of the tunnel, and higher still, at the peak of Mount Vesuvius, the thin finger of smoke had grown heavier. Dark bits of ash floated into the sky, and under my feet, deep in the earth, I felt the tremors and rumble of volcanic activity.

"*We are . . . unsure,*" the Board of the Winds said. "*Both of us have been asleep for many years. Too many possibilities exist for certainty. It is not, however, a name carried on any of the winds.*"

"*So much for that idea,*" I said, then turned my attention back to Peraud as we reached the opening.

"I don't suppose you have a flashlight or two handy," I said, peering into the dark tunnel. "There's not much light in there."

"I have no need for such tools," Peraud said. He

mumbled a few words, and a globe of light appeared in his hand. About the size of a basketball, it glowed like a streetlamp. "This will provide more than enough for our path."

"Neat trick," I said. "Do you pull rabbits out of your underwear, too?"

Peraud didn't answer my jibe, just handed me the glowing globe. "Take this," he said, "and keep going. Remember whose life you hold as well. Do not cross me, or Simon won't live to regret it."

"Fine," I said, holding the globe in both hands. It was cool to the touch and felt a little like one of those plasma lights you could buy in Radio Shack—the ones that arced blue and purple sparks from the center out to the glass where you touched it.

"That *is* a neat trick," I added, meaning it for once. "Could you teach me to do that?"

"Stop stalling and go!" Peraud snarled.

I guess it is too late to try and get on his good side, if there is one. "Sure, okay," I said. I took one last glance around, and that's when I saw her.

Amber. Creeping and crawling through the scrub and making her way to where we were. She was following, and that meant I had at least one more ally here. I didn't know what help she'd be, but I wasn't in a position to be picky about my friends at the moment.

Without another word, I stepped into the entrance,

holding the globe of light before me. Almost immediately, the tunnel narrowed and I saw that whoever had carved it must have used a spell of awesome power. It wasn't wide enough to allow more than one person through at a time, but the walls were as smooth as if they'd been carved by a laser.

About ten feet in, the tunnel turned sharply right and began to descend. The light illuminated enough of the way to show where the passage turned again and continued down even farther—into the very heart of the volcano itself, I suspected. The air smelled of sulfur and something else I couldn't readily identify, and it was very warm, almost hot.

Farther down, I knew, the air would become unbearably hot and probably unbreathable. Although the Board of the Winds would probably protect me, everyone else could die from the noxious fumes long before we reached the place where the Board was hidden. Realizing that I'd paused as the tunnel slanted down, I started moving again. As Peraud took great pleasure in reminding me, I had no choice.

I continued down, following the passage as it twisted and turned, and at one point, leveled off for a dozen paces before descending again. The air grew increasingly hot and difficult to breathe.

"Answer my summons, Board of the Winds," I called.

"What is your will, Keeper?"

"We need air," I said. *"Can you summon it from the surface?"*

"Your will is my will," it said.

The magical energy of the Board surged out, but before I knew it, I felt the cold steel kiss of a blade on my neck.

"What *are* you doing, Jenna?" Peraud hissed in my ear.

"Keeping us alive, you moron," I snapped, trying not to move. "I used the Board to summon fresh air from the surface. If we keep going like this, the fumes alone will kill us, or hadn't you noticed?"

The blade fell away and I took a deep breath, trying to remember that he didn't really *want* to kill me. He was, in effect, putting on a show. That didn't mean he wasn't willing to kill Simon or anyone else, but I had begun to think that Peraud was more talk than action. Something or someone held him back from truly harming me or Simon.

"Very well," Peraud said. "Warn me before you attempt to use the Boards again."

"Oh, I will," I said, trying to sound innocent and failing miserably.

"You don't have much respect for me, do you, Jenna?" Peraud asked.

"That's not true at all, Peraud," I said. "I do respect you—like I would any dangerous animal or a rabid dog."

From behind Peraud, I heard Simon say, "You know

what they do with rabid dogs, don't you, Peraud? They shoot them."

"You'll feel a bullet in your skull long before I do, *Brother*. Now both of you shut up and keep moving," he snarled, shoving me forward.

Far below, I could see where the tunnel ended.

The opening was the deep orange-red of lava and fire.

*"The Board is very close now, my Lord, almost
within my grasp. The very air is charged with its
energies."*

"What do you mean?"

*"I can sense the magic of the Board from here. It
is almost as if it is . . ."*

*"Already awakened! Control yourself, you fool. A
mistake at this juncture could prove fatal."*

The Board of the Winds heeded my call, and the air in
the tunnel swirled and became fresher as we descended. Eventually, though, even that grew stale, and
breathing grew more difficult as we got closer to the
end of our journey.

"Do you have any good magic tricks for keeping us
from suffocating while we're down here?" I asked Peraud. Somehow, knowing that he either didn't want to or

was somehow constrained from killing me—at least for now—had brought out what my grandfather had called the sass in me. I reached into the pocket of my jeans and pulled out the lining. "I'm fresh out."

"Yes," he muttered. Trying not to cough, he chanted under his breath for several long minutes, and suddenly the air was fresh, even sweet-smelling. All of us inhaled deeply, glad to have good air in our lungs again.

"You are just *full* of clever tricks, aren't you?" I asked. "I bet you're the life of every party."

"You might keep in mind that once we enter the primary chamber, the air will be toxic. The sphere of breathable air I've created isn't that large. If you get too far away from me—or if Simon happens to stumble—you'll be dead in minutes, perhaps only seconds. And that's assuming the heat doesn't sear your lungs closed first. From what I understand, it's not a pleasant way to go." Peraud grinned. "Stay close," he added, gesturing for me to continue.

I had to respect his persistence, if nothing else. Not a lot seemed to rattle him, and he was almost pathologically single-minded in his willingness to do whatever it took to get his hands on the Boards. Since that included hurting people I cared about, or the tens of thousands of innocents in this region who would die if we took the Board of the Flames, however, my respect was tempered quite a bit with anger.

I followed the last few feet of the tunnel to the cave opening and peered through, squinting my eyes against the dazzling intensity of the fire. We had to be almost in the center of the volcano. The heat was like a thick, invisible wall I had to push through, worse than the desert in Israel, worse than any hot day back home.

The chamber was massive, soaring overhead at least several hundred feet. The tunnel we'd been following opened onto a small ledge, and I stepped forward, handing the glowing ball of light back to Peraud, as there was plenty of light here now. He took it and clapped his hands together with the ball in between them, making it disappear in a quick flash of white.

The ledge we stood on was perhaps twenty feet wide and forty feet long—a natural shelf of rock that jutted out over a massive lake of lava. Gouts of flame shot into the air, and it bubbled and roiled like boiling water. In the center of the lake was a massive pillar of stone, rising out of the lava like a giant's forearm. On the top of the pillar, I saw a stone obelisk, and if I squinted my eyes through the smoke, I could make out the image of the nine-rayed Star of Chaos carved into it.

Even more disturbing, however, were the bones. Hundreds of human bones littered the ledge, and several partial skeletons dangled from the pillar itself.

"Our brother is very near, Keeper," the Board of the

Winds said. *"Though his attention is diverted elsewhere. That is why his call for us has been so quiet."*

I suddenly remembered something Dario had mentioned reading somewhere about the Board of the Flames. To awaken it, the surface of the Board must be touched by cremation fires. Cremation fires. I looked at all the bones littering the stone ledge and the pillar. This wasn't just a chamber for the Board, but had been used for the disposal of bodies for a long time.

The Board of the Flames had *never* gone quiet; it had been awake for all these years without a Keeper to control it. Which explained why Vesuvius had erupted more than thirty times over the last two centuries, and was building toward an eruption even now.

A huge gout of fire leapt out of the lake, splashing off the walls, and the voice of the Board—a roaring, searing menace—entered my mind.

"Greetings, Keeper. Have you come to master me?" It laughed, a sound like flames crackling in a hearth.

"I am the Keeper of the Boards," I replied. *"Your will is my will."*

More laughter. *"You are a pale shadow compared to Shalizander, the barest twitch of power compared to her daughter, Malizander. The bloodline has grown weak and useless, though I sense you have two of my brothers with you—Air and Water. The easiest of the Boards to control, Keeper. You will not find me nearly so willing."*

"What are you doing?" Peraud asked.

"Shut up. I'm speaking to the Board of the Flames," I said.

"Right now?" he asked, sounding strangely panicked. It occurred to me that Peraud hated losing control of events.

"No," I said. "It's happening tomorrow. Of course right now!"

"Stop," he said. "We'll take this a step at a time. I don't want you speaking to the Board just yet."

"It's your show," I said, shrugging. "So now what?"

Peraud examined the chamber carefully, assessing the situation with the same intense stare a hungry cat used on an unsuspecting mouse. He gestured to one of his men, and Simon was shoved forward.

"You will go and retrieve the Board of the Flames," he said to me, taking out his dagger and resting it easily beneath Simon's chin. "You will not use it in any way. Should anything go wrong . . ." He glanced meaningfully at the scattered bones. "Simon here will be the next in what has apparently been a long line of sacrifices made to this volcano."

"I'm going to need a few minutes," I said. "And my backpack."

"What for?" Peraud snapped.

"Because it's easier to use the Boards when I'm touching them," I explained. "Plus, as you so gleefully

JENNA SOLITAIRE

told me, if I leave the sphere you've created, I'll die, re-member? I'm going to have to figure out what to do about that *before* I go retrieve the Board."

Shrugging the backpack off his shoulder, Peraud tossed it to me. "Fine," he said. "Just remember that anything you do, I can *feel*, and if it doesn't feel right, Simon dies."

"So much for brotherly love," I said, sitting down on the stone shelf and opening the zipper on my battered backpack. I carefully removed the Boards and set them on my lap, then pulled out the Chronicle.

"Jenna, don't," Simon said. He was clearly exhausted, despair etched across his features. "It will only make you weak, and this isn't a good time for that."

"I know," I said. "But I don't even know *how* to get the Board of the Flames, and for that, I'm going to need to do a little digging."

I glanced at Peraud. "Do you understand how the Chronicle works?"

He shook his head. "Not exactly."

"When I read it, I see a vision of what the person wrote, only . . . in the first person. As though I am there. That can take time, so if it looks like I'm out of it, don't get hasty with that knife."

"Just get on with it, then," he said.

"One more thing," I added. "Reading it tends to make me pretty sick—you know that part—so I don't know what good I'm going to be when I finish."

Peraud pressed the point of the blade into the delicate skin of Simon's neck. "You better be good enough to finish the job. After all, you wouldn't want your usefulness to end too prematurely."

Around us, the walls shuddered. "And I wouldn't spend too long on your research if I were you," he added. "Time is running out."

I ignored him and opened the cover of the Chronicle without looking at any of the pages. I knew the Board of the Flames had caused the previous eruptions, and its nature would be to cause an eruption if I took it out of Mount Vesuvius—not for any other reason than it liked to burn things. Of the three Boards I had encountered so far, it was by far the most malevolent.

I had also lied to Peraud. I knew how to cross the lava and reach the pillar. That wasn't the problem I faced.

And there was no need to awaken the Board of the Flames—it was already awake—and so I had only to master it with my will. *That* was the problem. I knew the Board was strong-willed, strong enough to laugh at the notion of me mastering it. What I needed to know was its weakness, what would cause it to capitulate.

I turned a few pages into the text. What I needed to know, only Shalizander could tell me. I opened my eyes and began to skim, ignoring the snippets of vision that appeared in my mind, until I found what I wanted.

Opening myself up to the vision, I let Shalizander speak.

Everything I have tried has failed.

Each of the Boards seems to be impervious to any force I can wield, be it magical or mundane. Nothing has done anything more than irritate them or make them vindictive. Sometimes, they even find humor in what I attempt.

I look across the room at the workbench where the Boards are stacked in small alcoves, each one with a space of its own. I dare not combine them. That will only serve to make them stronger and more willful than they already are.

Once again, I ask myself: What do the Boards want?

The answer: the opening of the way. Something that will never happen as long as I live. So what do they fear? That the way will not be opened? No, they do not fear that.

Suddenly, it comes to me, and I leave my chair and cross the room. Beneath my worktable is a large, wooden chest. I open it and remove the few items within, then take down one of the Boards and put it in the trunk.

"What are you doing, Keeper?" the Board of the Flames rumbles in my mind. "What new game do you play?"

"No game," I tell it. "I'm putting the Boards away."

"Away?" the Board of the Winds asks. "What do you mean?"

"Away and gone," I say. "I'm through. Once I've loaded all of you into this trunk, I'm going to bury it beneath the tower and forget you exist."

"An artful jest, Keeper," the Board of the Waters says. "But you cannot forget us. You won't forget us."

"I will," I say. "I have the spell that will wipe all of you from my memory. I'm tired of it all."

"You do not mean this," the Board of the Flames says.

There is an urgency in its voice that is new to me. It is the urgency of fear.

"Yes, I do," I say. "I am going to put all of you away, forgotten forever by the human race and lost in the dark labyrinth beneath the tower."

"NO!" the Board of the Flames roars. "You must not!"

I stop what I am doing. "Why?" I ask it.

And it tells me.

I shook my head, the implication of the vision clear. I knew what the Board of the Flames feared, what all of the Boards feared. The only question now was how to use that, and I had an idea that might work, if I carried it off right.

"Jenna?" Simon asked. "Are you all right?"

I nodded and got slowly to my feet. The vision had been thankfully short, and the nausea wasn't as bad as the last time.

"Fine," I said, trying to control the weakness in my voice. "I've got to do this. It's our only chance."

"I know," he said. "You wouldn't be you if you didn't." His hands were still tied behind his back, and he did his best to smile. "Are you sure you know what you're doing?"

"Not really," I said. "But when do I ever?"

That got a genuine smile out of him, which was all I needed. I picked up the Chronicle and put it back in the pack, then hefted the Boards. "I'm ready," I said to Peraud.

"Then get going," he said.

"I am the Keeper of the Boards. Your will is my will. Hear my call and answer!"

I sent the mental command out to the Board of the Winds and the Board of the Waters, and both answered immediately.

"What is your will, Keeper?" they asked.

"I need a sphere of rain," I said, directing my thought to the Board of the Waters. *"Large enough to completely surround me."*

"There is a great deal of fire in this place, Keeper," it replied. *"Maintaining such a sphere will be difficult."*

"*Then call the rains! There must be an opening high above here, at the top of the volcano, else where did the bodies come from?*"

"*As you will, Keeper,*" it said.

I felt a magical surge lash out of the Board and up, higher and higher into the invisible realm of the shadowed ceiling.

"*I shall also need a wind, a cyclone like before, but much stronger,*" I said to the Board of the Winds. "*It must be strong enough to lift both me and the water sphere over the lava and to the pillar where your brother rests.*"

"*Your will is my will, Keeper,*" the Board of the Winds replied. "*There are enough thermals in this place to float you to the sky, should you wish it.*"

Remembering how it liked to caper on the winds, I said, "*Just to the pillar and back will do.*"

"*Yes, Keeper,*" it said.

I felt the Board of the Waters lash out once more and said, "Brace yourselves. We're about to get wet."

"*The storm comes, Keeper,*" the Board said.

"*Excellent. Form the sphere of water before me.*"

Raindrops began falling from above, many of them hissing into steaming oblivion before getting close, but slowly, more and more of them hit the ground. At my feet, a puddle began to take shape, rapidly forming into a small globe that grew larger by the minute.

Soon, a deluge of rain poured into the cavern, and clouds of steam began to rise from the lava as the droplets struck the fiery lake. Peraud muttered something, and the air around us shimmered as he strengthened the barrier he had created.

The sphere of water at my feet grew larger as the Board manipulated the rain, catching drop after drop and adding it to the whole. It was now almost half my height, shimmering and swirling in the red light of the cavern.

I felt a breeze stir against the skin of my face and knew that the Board of the Winds had begun calling on the thermals trapped within the cave.

"When I step into the sphere, use the winds to carry me to the pillar," I commanded the Board of the Winds.

"As you will, Keeper," it replied.

"Keep the rain coming," I said to the Board of the Waters. *"And don't let the sphere dissipate on the other side. Hold it together for as long as you can."*

"It shall be a shield of water, Keeper," the Board replied.

Hopeful that both Boards would keep their word, I reached out with my mind to the Board of the Flames.

"I am the Keeper of the Boards," I told it. *"Your will is my will. You* will *be mastered by me."*

"Come ahead then, mortal," it replied. *"And I shall offer you a kiss of flame for your trouble."*

I looked at the globe and knew the time had come. I could not drown—something I had learned shortly after I found the Board of the Winds in my grandfather's attic, when I'd been pitched into an icy river while tied hand and foot. At the bottom, I found that I could breathe just like normal.

The magic of the Board would protect me here, too, but if I faltered or the Boards betrayed me, there would be no turning back. I'd plunge into the lake of lava below and have about a millisecond to say my prayers before I died.

I looked at Simon, and he nodded solemnly. He knew that whatever I was going to do, it would be dangerous. Peraud made a "move it along" wave that I found incredibly irritating. If he was such a talented wizard, why wasn't *he* floating up there to get the Board of the Flames?

As the question crossed my mind I stopped myself from stepping into the sphere of water. *Why wasn't he going after it?*

What was I missing? Any other time, Peraud would already have the Board in his greedy clutches . . . or would he? I searched my mind, and the solution snapped into place like a puzzle piece. It was the one thing I'd never seen Peraud do, and I stored this knowledge away for use in the near future.

Everyone has a weakness, I reminded myself.

I stepped into the sphere of water and at once felt that strange sensation of bubbles rising out of my chest. The water was cold, but not as frigid as the river had been, and it was warming rapidly in the air of the volcano.

"Call the winds," I said to the Board of the Winds. *"Lift me up to the top of the pillar."*

"Your will is my will, Keeper," it replied.

I saw, rather than felt, the thermals stir, and almost immediately the globe began to lift.

"How very clever of you, Keeper," the Board of the Flames said. *"Do you think it will be enough to save you?"*

I felt the sphere totter and then steady as the winds increased and I flew up and out over the lake of lava. I could look down and see it.

"Protect me from what?" I shot back, trying to focus on the winds, keeping them moving me forward and up, as fast as possible, while directing the Board of the Waters to keep replenishing the sphere with more rains.

"Fire is a living element, Keeper," it rumbled. *"Do you know that it mimics life itself?"*

"How's that?" I asked, urging the winds to go faster, sensing that the Board of the Flames meant to harm me before I could get to it.

"It breathes oxygen, it grows, it multiplies . . . and it eats!" the Board roared.

All around me, massive tongues of flame and molten rock leaped into the air.

I couldn't dodge them, and that's when I knew that everyone has a weakness and mine was most definitely overconfidence.

"I can feel your fear, Keeper, and it feels good to me," the Board of the Flames said. *"Come closer and allow me to give you my promised kiss—the last one you will ever feel."*

"I will have the Board within moments, my Lord. The Keeper is retrieving it, even as we speak."

"The Keeper? You are a fool! The Board is awakened, and she will turn its powers against you."

"Not this time, my Lord. I hold her heart in my hands. She is weak, as we have suspected, and that weakness has made her my puppet."

"You'd better hope so, Peraud. For your sake, I hope you haven't underestimated her."

"*Strengthen the sphere!*" I ordered the Board of the Waters seconds before a gout of lava surged up and hit the bottom of the globe.

Instantly, the water boiled around me, and a cloud of steam rose as the liquid from the bottom evaporated into scalding-hot steam.

A powerful deluge of rain washed over the sphere,

ten thousand droplets hitting at once and cooling the air around me. But would it be enough?

"Faster!" I urged the Board of the Winds.

The sphere floated forward more quickly, but the Board of the Flames wasn't done yet. More bursts of molten rock leaped into the air at us.

"Don't let the lava hit us," I ordered the Board of the Winds. *"And keep the rain coming!"* I added to the Board of the Waters.

Another wave of lava splattered upon the sphere, and the water below me boiled once more. As before, the Board of the Waters responded with a massive downpour of raindrops, replacing the boiling water in an instant.

The top of the pillar came into view, and in another moment it was beneath me. I stepped out of the sphere.

"Well done, Keeper," the Board of the Flames said. *"Still, you will not master me with your will."*

"Probably not," I admitted. *"But I don't have to."*

"If you do not seek to master me, why are you here?"

"To destroy you," I said, striving to keep calm. *"If I cannot bind you to me, then I will ensure that your powers are not used by anyone else."*

The Board of the Flames roared laughter, the crackling sound almost deafening, even in the volcano. *"Oh, Keeper, you amuse me. We cannot be destroyed by any means you possess."*

I looked around. Skeletal remains littered the top of the pillar, and I wondered how many bodies had been disposed of here, and how many had still been alive when they were tossed into the chasm. The Board was situated on a small pedestal of rock and looked much like the other two Boards: triangular in shape, with one side cut out like a crescent that dipped lower and reached a point. The symbols scored into its surface were clearly in the same language as, but quite different from those on the other Boards in my possession. All of them seemed to be different representations of fire.

"I don't mean destruction in the physical sense," I said.

"Then what is your intention, Keeper?"

I picked up the Board of the Flames and immediately felt my skin begin to burn. I only had a few seconds before my skin would blister and render my hands useless.

"I will cast you into the lava below, where you will be lost and unused for all eternity and the way will not be opened!"

"NO!" all three Boards shouted at once.

I stepped toward the edge, trying to ignore the searing pain in my hands, and held the Board out over the lava. The burning was intense, but I gritted my teeth and held on. Across the chasm, I heard Peraud yelling, but my attention was focused solely on the hot Board in my grasp.

"I will do it!"

"You must stop her!" the Board of the Flames roared.

"We cannot! You must submit!" the other two Boards shouted, the conversation deafening in my mind.

"I will not *submit to another Keeper! I will cause this volcano to erupt as it did when first I was placed in this prison, and all will die, swept away in fire and lava!"*

"Do it," I said, gambling everything on being right. "Go ahead and destroy us all, losing yourself in the process!"

"No!" the Board of the Winds screeched. *"All will be lost and the way will not be opened! Brother, you must submit!"*

A long moment of silence stretched out, and then the Board began to cool in my throbbing hands. *"Say it,"* I said. *"Say it now."*

"I submit," the Board of the Flames rumbled.

"No," I said. "You know what you must say."

The angry roar of a forest fire filled my mind for a second, and then, *"You are the Keeper of the Boards. Your will is my will. Call to me—and I am yours."*

"Board of the Flames, I am the Keeper of the Boards. Come to me. Your will is my will, and our hungers are as one."

"I hear, Keeper," the Board of the Flames said. *"I hear and obey."*

Reminding myself that the Boards could not be trusted, especially the Board of the Flames, I moved away from the edge of the pillar and removed my backpack. The heat was still immense, but the Board protected me, and the constant stream of rain was also helping to keep it bearable, if just barely. I held up the two combined Boards and peered at the edges, then brought the Board of the Flames closer and slipped it into place. The three Boards were now combined as one, and unless the fourth Board was differently shaped, they weren't going to fit together correctly.

I wondered if we weren't missing some key piece of knowledge, but then shook my head. This wasn't the time for pondering what might or might not be. I somehow had to save Simon and get us out of here alive and with the Boards.

"You must not allow the volcano to erupt," I commanded the Board of the Flames.

"But the fires . . ." the Board replied.

"No," I said. *"The natural order of things must be restored. You have disturbed them long enough."*

I was sure the Board wanted to argue, wanted to fight me, but it was bound to obey my will. But just in case it didn't get it, I added, *"The volcano must not erupt,"*

"Your will is my will, Keeper," it said.

"Good," I said. *"Try to remember that in the future."*

The Board didn't offer a reply, but already I could hear its voice joined in conversation with the other two.

The combined Boards now looked like a star missing

some of its points, and I shoved them into the backpack. The configuration was more awkward, but keeping them together *felt* right to me. I wondered how I was going to manage more than four of them—assuming, of course, I survived this venture to even collect the others.

"Call the thermals once more," I commanded the Board of the Winds. *"I must float back down to the ledge."*

The Board didn't reply, but I felt the thermals stirring as I stepped back into the sphere of water. A minute later it lifted into the air and began the slow descent back to the rock shelf where Peraud and the others waited.

This time as we crossed, the lava looked more like a red lake than anything else, its surface ashy and still. The Board of the Flames was keeping its word so far. I floated down within the sphere and landed gently on the stone ledge, then stepped out of the water. The sphere fell apart behind me with a gurgling splash, and the rain stopped.

"Well?" Peraud asked. "Did you get it?"

I nodded. "Yes." I looked at Simon. "Are you all right?"

"I could use a hot shower and a meal, but other than that—"

Peraud's blade flicked upward and cut off Simon's

words as the point sank into the skin under his jaw. "No more fun and games," he said. "Let's see them."

I pulled my backpack off my shoulders and set it at my feet. "Go ahead," I said. "Look for yourself."

"Jenna, what are you doing?" Simon said. "Have you lost your mind?"

"Simon, please be quiet," I said very softly. "You can scold me all you want later."

"Open it," Peraud said. "And take out the Boards."

I shook my head. "No, Peraud. I got them for you, but I won't be your servant. If you want them, they're right there in the backpack."

"You could've put anything in there," he snapped.

I could hear the fear in his tone, and I smiled, knowing that I had figured out something important. I used my foot to nudge the backpack closer.

"What, a rock? A lava snake? There's nothing in there but the Boards, the Chronicle, and my BlackBerry," I said. "Go on and see for yourself."

Peraud's eyes narrowed. "You've figured it out, I see," he said.

I nodded, but kept my silence.

"Open the pack and show me the Boards," he said. "Or I'll kill Simon right now."

Sighing, I picked up the pack and unzipped it. I then held it open for him to look inside. "See?" I said.

Greed lit his features—three of the four Boards were

within his grasp, but for one problem. He couldn't touch them! I'd never once seen him physically touch one of the Boards, and for whatever reason he didn't want to. It was the ultimate irony.

"I don't understand," Simon said.

Peraud ignored him. "Zip it up and slip the strap over my shoulder," he said.

"Jenna, don't," Simon said. "You can't let him have them."

"You must be ready to die, Brother," Peraud said. "Are all your causes so just?"

"We may be brothers by blood," Simon said, "but that is all we share, and all we ever will. It must be terribly lonely out there in the darkness."

I could see that Simon's remark hit a nerve, as Peraud's jaw muscles twitched.

"Shut up," he snarled. "Jenna, zip up the pack and put it on my shoulder—now!"

He was practically screaming, and I wondered for a moment if the excitement of his triumphant moment wasn't going to do us all a favor and give him a nice, convenient heart attack or stroke.

"Fine, fine," I said, zipping the pack closed. "There's no need to get your knickers in a twist."

"Jenna . . . ." Simon started to say, but my gaze cut him off.

"It will be fine," I said. "Trust me."

The last time I'd asked him to trust me, he said he did and I had pushed him off the edge of a cliff. For a moment, I wondered if he knew what I was telling him, but then he nodded slightly and I was satisfied.

"Here you go, Peraud. Your moment of triumph. All your machinations and hard work are about to be rewarded." I slipped the strap of the pack over his shoulder and backed away.

"You've got the Boards, but you can't touch them, so now what are you going to do?" I asked.

Peraud grinned and shoved Simon to his knees. Then he turned to his men. "Kill the priest. Bring the woman along—we have other uses planned for her."

As I thought, no matter how evil Peraud thought he was, he wouldn't kill his own brother. Ordering others to do it apparently wasn't a problem, however. Glancing into the passageway, I saw what I had hoped to see. The golden gleam of an eye.

"Amber, now!" I shouted, diving for where Simon knelt on the floor.

Peraud looked around for the threat he assumed was coming, turning just as the German shepherd jumped at him, jaws clamping on his throat. A gurgling scream sounded from beneath the mound of writhing fur as he flew backward, arms and legs flailing.

I pulled Simon to his feet as Peraud's guards closed in. I picked up the backpack where it had landed. "Stay close to me, Simon," I muttered. "I don't know how all this is going to work quite yet."

One of Peraud's guards grabbed Amber and bodily pulled her off the struggling sorcerer. She continued to snap and bite even as he threw her into the passageway, where she landed with a sharp crack and a yelp of pain.

"Stay, Amber!" I called out, hoping the noise I heard wasn't the sound of her spine breaking against the rock.

Peraud struggled to his feet, blood rushing from the wounds on his throat, face, and arms. "You'll pay for that," he said, gasping for air. "Oh, you'll pay for a long, long time."

"Who's going to make me pay, Peraud?" I asked. "You? You won't kill me—I may not know who holds your leash, but I know the rules he's making you play by."

The look in his eyes was enough to convince me that maybe I'd gone too far. He wasn't just angry; he was enraged. Quite literally spitting blood. He raised his hands and muttered an incantation. A shower of sparks flew out from his closed fists, and in seconds the wounds on his throat were gone as though they had never been there.

"So," he said. "The Keeper thinks she's all grown up now and ready to play with the adults?"

I'd come this far, and my choices were limited. I didn't believe I'd made a mistake in my judgment of his situation. I edged backward, well aware that the ledge had limited space, no cover, and a lake of fiery lava on one side, Peraud and his men blocking the other.

"I'm ready to play with you, Peraud," I called. "But I don't think you're prepared for me. I may as well be a human Board to you—you can't touch me, can you?"

Shoving his guards aside, Peraud stepped forward. There was an insanity in his eyes that I didn't like, but scaring him and making him lose control had been part of my hastily-conceived plan.

"What's it like, always having to take orders from someone else, Peraud? Never getting to do things your way? Never getting a taste of that power you've worked so long and so hard to possess."

Peraud began laughing, and it sounded like a man swallowing broken glass.

"He's gone over the edge," Simon muttered in my ear, guiding my backward steps with his hand. "Be very careful with what you say now."

"I know, I know," I whispered. "But this time I've actually got a plan, you know."

"Really? What is it?"

"I'm sort of making it up as I go along," I admitted, turning my attention back to Peraud.

"You think my master keeps me on a short leash?" Peraud asked. "Well, you're right; he does. But not this time. This time, I will kill you, Jenna Solitaire."

"And how will you explain that to your master?" I called. "I'm sure he knows that yapping dogs are capable of telling lies."

"I won't be explaining anything to him," Peraud sneered. "With the three Boards in my power, I will be untouchable. I will be the most powerful sorcerer on the face of the Earth!"

"Wow," Simon muttered. "You've really unbalanced him."

"Get ready," I said. "It's about to start."

"What?" Simon asked.

"I'm going to finish Peraud," I said. "Once and for all."

"No, Jenna," he said. "Just . . . just get us out of here. We'll fight him another day."

"There aren't going to be any other days, Simon," I said. "It ends here and now. I won't spend the rest of my life wondering which shadow he's going to jump out of next."

Simon must have heard the determination in my voice, because he didn't argue. He simply said, "I'm with you, and I'll do anything I can to help."

"Good," I muttered. I stepped away from Simon and toward Peraud.

"All right, Peraud," I called. "If you've truly slipped your master's leash, prove it. Let's finish this thing, right here and right now. No more games, and no more chasing each other around the planet."

"I don't need these fools around me to destroy you! I'll enjoy doing it myself!" Peraud answered, hurling a lightning bolt that barely missed me and sheared off a piece of rock with a thunderous explosion. It splashed into the lava and disappeared with a quick flare as it melted.

Apparently, he was as serious as I was. I backed up a step and called on the Boards, wondering how I was going to defeat him.

That was when I heard a new voice in my mind and for a second wondered if I'd gone crazy.

"Jenna, if you're going to defeat Peraud, you'll need help."

"Who are you?"

"I am the one you call Amber, though that is not my human name."

Thinking of the dog's yelp, I said, *"Are you all right?"*

"I cannot walk properly. My back legs are broken."

"I'm sorry," I said.

"Do not be sorry. I am keeping the promise made to Malizander."

"Thank you," I said.

"If you die here, the promise will not be fulfilled; our spirits will still be trapped."

Peraud tossed another bolt of lightning my way, and Simon and I both ducked as it flew past.

"I'm open to ideas," I thought.

"Malizander left something else in this chamber besides the Board," Amber said. An image of the dagger filled my mind. It was hidden below the stone where the Board of the Flames had been.

"Would have been good to know that earlier!" I thought as Peraud continued his slow advance, tossing bolt after bolt of lightning.

A faint sound like laughter, then, *"I thought you already knew."*

"Keeper," the Board of the Winds interjected. *"Time is of the essence. Peraud is not in his right mind, and he will kill you if he is given the chance."*

"Thank you, Amber," I said.

"Save us all, Keeper," she replied; then she was gone again.

I reached out with my mind to the Board of the Flames. *"Hear my summons and answer my call, Board of the Flames."*

"What is your will, Keeper?" it asked in its rumbling voice.

"Can you protect me from fire the way your brothers can lend aid with their element?"

"Of course," the Board of the Flames replied. *"All natural fires are subject to my powers."*

Another attack from Peraud, this time in the form of a

fireball. His aim was terrible, and I suspected it was because he kept laughing. He was also crying.

"And can you work in concert with your brothers?"

"So long as we are combined, yes," it replied.

"That's good," I said. *"Get ready, then."*

"What is your will, Keeper?" the Board of the Waters asked.

"Call on the winds, call on the rain, and call on the flames. All the elements must be at my command," I told them, while simultaneously pushing Simon toward the edge of the rock shelf.

"Jenna, what are you doing?" he asked. "We're getting awful close to the lava."

"Your will is our will, Keeper," the Boards replied in unison.

Peraud saw what I was doing and increased the pace of his lightning bolts, spearing them at us so rapidly it was like standing in a fireworks show. Every now and then, one would look like it was going to hit us, and then it would bounce off in another direction.

"Are you doing that?" I asked Simon.

"Doing what?" he said.

"Making him miss like that?"

"It's not me," he said. "I thought it was you."

The rains came back with a vengeance then, and the thermals in the cavern began swirling madly. At my back, the lava began boiling once more. It rose up behind me and Simon like a wall of red-orange blood from the very heart of the Earth itself.

"Lift us up!" I said to the Board of the Winds.

Simon and I floated upward, soaked in a rainfall that kept us wet and cool.

"Get ready," I said to the Board of the Flames. A wave of glowing lava rose from the lake, undulating and popping.

I pointed at where Peraud was standing, still hurling lightning bolts at us and wondering what was making them miss. *"Consume them,"* I ordered.

"Your will is my will, Keeper," the Board of the Flames said, pure, malevolent glee in its voice.

The wave of lava crashed forward and down, and it was then I realized that Peraud's men hadn't spoken once in all the time I'd spent with them. Their odd-sounding screams provided an explanation—they didn't have their tongues. *What kind of a man cut the tongues out of his servants?* I wondered, but the answer came to me: a man who didn't want his servants to speak about what they might know. He had protected himself from betrayal, even as he was preparing to betray his own master.

The last thing I saw of Peraud was him hurling one final bolt of lightning as the lava descended on him, the look on his face a mix of terror and fury that I hoped I would never see again.

The lava wave splashed against the side of the cavern, coating the ledge in thick globs of molten rock, then drifted back and settled into the lake once more. The shelf remained, but now it was as devoid of life as stone could be.

Peraud and all his men were finally gone.

13

"Already the Keeper has gotten farther than I ever dared dream. Perhaps she is truly the one foretold by prophecy, the one who shall open the way after all these long centuries of trying . . . and failing. Which reminds me that I'd best go and retrieve that failure, Peraud. It seems as though the old clichés are the best ones: if you want something done right, do it yourself."

I used the Board of the Winds to float us up to the top of the stone pillar. There was an odd silence in the chamber as we settled to the ground near the stone where I'd mastered the Board of the Flames.

"He's dead," Simon said.

"Yes," I said. "Even for Peraud, I'm sorry."

"He'd slipped over the edge into madness, and no matter who his master was, he would have killed us both this time. You did what was necessary." He stepped toward me and wrapped me in a hug. "Are you all right?"

I buried my face in his chest and nodded, not trusting myself to speak. So much had happened in a few hours—Dario had died, and I had killed several men. What did that make me? The whole sequence of events since we'd entered the volcano seemed like a terrible dream that I couldn't wake up from.

"Let's get out of here," Simon said.

I nodded again and moved to the stone where the Board had been placed. Searching it carefully, I found a large rectangle of rock that was slightly out of place, and gripped the edges with my fingers. With an odd scraping sound of two lava rocks rubbing together, it came free. I set the stone aside and reached into the space behind it, reminded of the day, not too long ago, when I had pulled free a brick from the pedestal of the statue at St. Anne's and found the Chronicle.

Inside the opening, I felt the outlines of a small box and pulled it out. The wood glowed in the red light of the cavern, its surface undamaged by the intense heat and the long years it had been sitting here. It was marked with runes similar to those on the Boards.

"What do you have there, Jenna?" Simon asked from behind me.

I saw the brass catch and opened it, hearing Simon's sharp gasp at what lay within.

Inside was the dagger Malizander had used to absorb Shalizander's soul and magic. The dagger she had then plunged into her own chest to create a bond between them. The dagger that could not be broken. Even to my untrained eye, I could sense the aura of power surrounding the ancient blade. It was a living thing, and I wasn't quite sure what I wanted to do with it.

I lifted it free of the box and saw a hand-tooled leather sheath beneath it. I slipped the blade into the sheath and strapped it onto my belt, then put the box in my backpack.

"What is that thing, Jenna?" Simon asked. "It felt . . . almost alive."

"It is the blade of Shalizander," I said shortly. "I'll tell you more about it later. Let's get out of here."

"I couldn't agree more," he said.

I called on the Board of the Winds, and it lifted us once more across the lava and onto the stone ledge, where we made our way into the tunnel. Amber was waiting for us, her back legs twisted beneath her, but her tail still gamely wagging all the same.

"Hello, Amber," I said. *"Are you well?"*

She whined once, and I heard her say, *"I do not wish to be left in this dark place. Please."*

"Simon, will you carry her?" I asked. "Be gentle. Her legs are broken."

For once, he didn't speak or ask questions. Maybe he was too tired. Or maybe he had finally accepted that something about the dog was different. Without a word, he knelt and picked her up, and she only whined once as he settled her into his arms.

"Let's go," he said, starting back up the tunnel.

It would have been nice to have a light, since the tunnel was narrow and steep. We slowly picked our way toward the surface, pausing to rest from time to time and not speaking much. I started thinking about Shalizander and Malizander . . . and the dream I'd had the night we first arrived in Pompeii.

The dream in which a young woman had possessed the Boards of Air, Water, and Fire, and all three had turned on her. If Malizander had hidden the Board of the Flames in Mount Vesuvius, then who had the girl been? How had she gotten the Boards, and how had the Board been returned to the inside of the volcano? Yet another unexplained mystery, and I sighed in weary frustration. There was always something to be figured out, but never enough information to answer the endless questions, and just once it would be nice to go to sleep at night without worrying about much of anything.

We reached the top of the passageway and stepped

out into the fading sunlight of late afternoon. Short of causing another rockslide, there was no way to seal off the passage, so we left it alone. No doubt some wanderer would find it and people would explore it and wonder what it had been for, and who had created it.

After a short rest, I said, "We've got to make a cairn for Dario. We can't just leave him out here."

"Absolutely," Simon said. "It's the least we can do. When we get back to Pompeii, I'll send someone to recover the body and arrange for a proper burial."

We started back down the broken trail, and I realized that I hadn't spoken very much and that I didn't want to. Mostly what I wanted to do was sleep. Going down takes a lot less time than climbing up, and we reached the spot where Dario's body lay. Simon set Amber down on a flat rock and came to stand near me.

I stood looking down at the old priest who had served the Templars to his last breath. He had tried to help me, and it had cost him his life.

"He was thrilled to have met you, Jenna," Simon said, putting an arm around my shoulders. "He told me that, told me how glad he was to be useful again."

Dashing away the tears that were running down my face, I said, "Then why did he have to die, Simon? He was a harmless old man and you—I'm sorry, I mean Peraud—killed him. He never had a chance."

"No, he didn't," Simon said. "But he would be proud

of what you accomplished here today. You've got the Board of the Flames, and you kept Vesuvius from erupting. You also found another magical artifact, Shalizander's dagger, that I didn't even know existed." He pulled me closer and gently turned my chin to look up at him. "And you saved my life."

In his eyes, I could see everything I'd longed to see there—love, passion, commitment, hope—and I knew that he was going to kiss me again. Like he had in Petra. That it would feel like coming home. He leaned forward, and I closed my eyes, preparing for that jolt of recognition and that warm, "soaking in a hot bath," loved feeling I remembered.

Suddenly, I heard a loud zapping noise and Simon was literally blasted out of my arms. My skin tingled, as if we had just shared the mother of all static shocks.

I jerked open my eyes and saw Simon lying prone on the ground, his clothes smoldering. He didn't move. And beyond him. . . .

Peraud, scorched and burned, but still very much alive.

He held his hands about a foot apart, and I saw small currents of pure electricity arc between them.

"That should take care of my dear brother for a while," Peraud said, stepping forward. "I'll deal with him shortly—after I'm finished with you once and for all,

Keeper." He flexed his fingers, and the bolts between them arced and snapped, discharging into the ground.

I snapped my mouth closed and tried to shake off the shock. "You're tougher than you look," I said. "I figured you were dead. How is it that you keep turning up like this?"

He held up the necklace he wore—the one that matched Simon's. "A magical gift of sorts, a family heirloom. It allowed me to track every move Simon made—and where he went, you went. It also allows for short distance jumps in space, commonly called teleporting. Convenient, wouldn't you say?"

"There's nothing about you that's convenient, Peraud. I'm going to finish you this time."

"I'm hard to kill. Better people than you have tried," he replied.

"Daughter, let him get close. He doesn't know about the dagger."

"Who? What?"

"No time. Let him get close, then strike!"

I took a few steps closer, trying to buy time.

"We don't have to be enemies, Peraud," I said. "Go back to your master and tell him I escaped. He's got to be used to disappointment by now."

"He doesn't take disappointment well at all," Peraud said, the electricity buzzing and crackling in front of him. "But this isn't about him. It's about me. The power should be mine!" The electricity jumped and arced more loudly. "And I don't take disappointment well either!"

He pointed his hands toward me, and the current leaped through the air. My whole body stiffened as electricity coursed through me, like I'd stuck my fist in a gigantic light socket. My teeth gritted together and then. . . .

"Keeper, such energies are easily dissipated by my powers," the Board of the Waters said.

The sensation passed at the same moment as I heard, *"Excellent. Continue to act as though you are suffering from the effects of the shock."*

That was easy enough to do considering that it felt like my muscles were ready to jump out of my skin. I kept my body stiff, my jaws clenched. Peraud lifted his hands, and I stumbled to the ground.

"Hurts, doesn't it?" he sneered, walking over to stand over me.

"Now, Daughter! Strike now!"

I let myself go limp and drew the dagger from my belt at the same time. Peraud's eyes widened in surprise, and he said, "What?"

Then I slammed the dagger into his abdomen with all my strength.

Peraud grabbed at his stomach, and the currents of electricity faded into the air. He staggered back a few steps, staring at the dagger protruding from his body in shock. "How did you do that?" he whispered.

"That's for Dario," I hissed.

He was a dead man, and we both knew it. I took a step back, and then the whole scene seemed to freeze, like a still-frame picture. Next to Peraud, a black outline appeared in the air, like the crack of an open doorway into darkness, and a robed form stepped through. A night-black hand shot forward and grasped the sorcerer by the wrist. Peraud screamed once in agony and then slumped to the ground.

The robed form turned in my direction. No face or even skin was visible, and a long second passed as it stared at me. That was when I realized that for all its apparent solidity, I could see *through* the being that stood before me.

A heavy, masculine voice sounded in my mind as it stared at me.

"So, you are the one. The last Keeper of the Boards and the last of the Solitaire line. The so-called 'Daughter of Destiny.'"

The figure reached out and plucked the dagger from Peraud's abdomen, ignoring the shudder that coursed through the wizard's body.

I didn't know what to say or if I should even speak, but before I could do anything, the voice continued.

"I haven't seen this dagger in many hundreds of years.

227

It has powers far beyond its keen edge, and those abilities allowed it to slice through his magical shields. That alone would cause him great agony for many days, but Peraud has too often disappointed me and will pay for his failures. Your time, however, has not yet come, young Jenna Solitaire, but it will. Our destinies are as intertwined as the paths of the stars themselves.

"*Interesting,*" the figure added, still holding the keen blade aloft. "*I had long wondered how she did that.*" He threw the dagger, which spun end over end to pierce the ground at my feet. "*Keep it. Consider it compensation for the loss of your great-grandfather, Dario, who died in service to your cause. You will need it again, I assure you. You are not yet ready to face me, but when that time comes, remember that I chose to allow you to live today. You do not know the rules of the game we play, but you will learn. In time, you will learn.*"

With that, it reached down and lifted Peraud's body effortlessly off the ground and turned back to the doorway. "*Farewell, Keeper. We* will *meet again.*" Then it stepped through the doorway and was gone.

I looked around the quiet landscape and saw that Simon was stirring, groaning weakly. I bent down and picked up the dagger, and ignored the voice that whispered, "*Well done, my daughter.*" I slipped it back into the sheath, and ran to where Simon was trying to sit up.

"What happened?" he asked. "Are you all right?"

"Peraud," I said, kneeling next to him. "He wasn't quite as dead as we thought."

Simon looked around wildly. "Where is he? Where'd he go?"

I shook my head. "He's gone," I said. "Gone forever."

"Gone?"

"I killed him, Simon—or may as well have. Either way, at least *he* won't be bothering us in the future."

Quietly, Simon said, "He was my brother."

"I know," I said. "But I wouldn't change the outcome for the world." I reached out and clasped the chain of the necklace, giving it a hard yank. The chain broke, and I placed it in Simon's hand. "You can't wear this anymore, Simon. It allows Peraud's master to track you."

Shaking his head, Simon said, "I . . . I didn't know." He stared at the coin in his palm for a long moment, then shook his head. "It seems I am denied even the one heirloom I had." He threw the necklace into a cluster of nearby rocks. "But at least you are safe and Peraud can no longer threaten us." He started to ask another question, and I shushed him.

"No, Simon. I'm tired, you're hurt, and we've got a lot yet to do. It's going to be night soon, and we still have to bury Dario." *My great-grandfather. That's what that . . . thing said.*

"Yes, but. . . ." he started to say. Then, seeing the look on my face, he nodded.

"Thank you," I said, helping him to his feet.

I didn't want to talk, and a few minutes later, when Simon started to say something, all I said was, "Please, Simon. We'll talk later. Let's just finish what we have to do."

I was emotionally exhausted. While Amber watched quietly, Simon and I built a cairn over Dario's body, doing what we could to keep it safe from scavengers and the elements. When it was finished and a crude marker of stone was put in place, I asked Simon to say a prayer.

He nodded, and I bowed my head as he spoke words from memory and finished by saying, "From dust we spring forth, and to dust we return. Yet Your holy word promises us that no one is ever truly gone. Lord, we ask that You help us to find comfort in knowing that our good friend Dario is not gone either. He is lost to our sight, but not our hearts, and though there are times when we are surrounded by darkness and death, and the lamp of Your glory shines dimly, we know that in Your plan and with Your promise, we will all find each other again in Heaven. Amen."

Goodbye, Great-grandfather. A single tear trickled down my cheek.

"Amen," I said.

It was almost completely dark by then. Simon picked up Amber, and in silence, stepping with care on the areas of loose stone that littered the mountainside, we made our way down to where the truck had been parked. Above us, Mount Vesuvius was quiet again, and I imagined that the people of this valley were breathing a collective sigh of relief, never knowing how truly close they had come to complete destruction.

Simon put Amber on an old blanket in the back of the truck and climbed into the driver's seat. The keys were thankfully still in the ignition, and the vehicle started easily. He turned it around and pointed it back down the road toward Pompeii.

When he turned on the headlights, only one of them worked, and we followed the single ray of light into the darkness. I knew we had to talk, but somehow, I just didn't have the strength or the energy to deal with it.

I leaned my head back and closed my eyes, and heard Simon whisper, "Get some rest, Jenna. I'll wake you when we get there."

I took his advice and drifted into sleep.

The Tower stands alone, floating above the red desert sands, a marker to a forgotten civilization that once created magics undreamed of.

I follow the spiral stairs up and up until I reach the

door to her room. I know she is on the other side, waiting for me, yet . . . to reach out and open that door, to cross the threshold, will mean a step taken that cannot be untaken.

I don't know who I am now . . . or what I may become if I take that step.

"Daughter, don't delay. Time does not pass here as it does in the real world."

I open the door and see her. She sits by the window that once overlooked the city. She looks like me, like my mother, and my grandmother and my great-grandmother . . . the circle opens and closes in the blink of an eye.

"Come," she says. "Come and sit with me. I have waited for you for a long time."

Doubting, I cross the threshold and sit in the chair next to her. A breeze comes in through the window and ruffles her hair.

This is not the Shalizander who died—this is the Shalizander who lived. Her power radiates from her like the aura of the sun.

"Your name is Jenna," she says. "And you are my ultimate daughter. The line ends with you, the prophecy fulfilled."

"You are Shalizander," I say. "My ultimate mother. The line began with you. And this huge, unbelievable mess you left behind."

Sorrow softens her features, and she nods once in ac-knowledgment. "As much of the responsibility is mine as it was Malkander's . . . and the others who helped us create the Boards. Power creates arrogance, child, as much as and perhaps more than it creates corruption."

"What is this place?" I ask.

"It is a construct," she says. "A dream world I created to capture my soul so that one day I could live again . . . to right the wrongs I left for you."

"Live again?"

"Through you, Daughter," she says. "You saw what Malizander did with the dagger. For long years, she car-ried my spirit and knowledge within herself."

"And you want me to do the same?"

Shalizander nodded. "Yes, Daughter. I can help you gather the Boards and contain their evil. Though the magic in my blood has grown weak with the centuries, within you I can strengthen it, giving you skills you haven't yet dreamed of."

"And the price?" I ask.

She smiles. "Yes, there is always a price, Daughter," she says. "But the compensation of my aid will be worth much to you in the coming days. You battle a foe more deadly than Peraud. His master's powers are so vast that even with all thirteen Boards in your possession, you would find him a mortal challenge."

"Who is he?" I ask.

"He is the undying mage. He is the one who does not sleep and who is constrained by his master to open the way. He is Malkander—my lover and my betrayer."

"And my ultimate father?"

"Yes," she says. "But unlike myself, he has never died, though he should have during the creation of the Boards. Instead, he made a deal for immortality with the entity that tricked us, and the price was his soul."

"Malkander is still alive?" I ask. "After . . . thousands of years?"

She nods, her red hair a shimmering crown of fire. "He lives, and he plots for you and against you. His machinations have spanned the centuries, and now that the prophecy nears its fruition, he will move to ensure that his vision of it comes true. As my line has borne daughters, so has he borne sons to aid him in his plans."

Stunned, I sit in silence, thinking of the implications. If Peraud's master was Malkander, and Simon was Peraud's brother, then . . .

I look up, and Shalizander's gaze meets my own. "Yes," she says. "Malkander is their father."

"No," I gasp. "No, that cannot be! How could something so evil have spawned such good?"

"The prophecy," Shalizander says, getting to her feet and turning to look out the window. "We are as trapped by it as the stars are in their courses—and all of us are *subject to our own prophecies. Once every one hundred years, Malkander fathers a child, but his prophecy says that in the time when he fathers two children, twins, will the opening of the way be nigh. When Simon and Peraud were born, Malkander sent them to orphanages—he has never had a use for young children.*

"Peraud showed an early talent for magic, while Simon—"

"Was taken in by the faith of the Church," I finish.

"Yes," she says. "But you must not tell Simon this. Not yet. It would break him. Already he struggles to balance his faith in God and his love for you."

"Tell me something I don't know," I say. "So what now?"

"You must use the dagger as Malizander did," she says. "Fear not. The magic will sustain your life. Once you have done so, you and I will be one—my knowledge will be yours and yours mine."

I am reminded of the ritual words of awakening the Boards, and I say, "And the price."

"What matters the price," she snaps, her beautiful features darkening with anger, "to save the world from the opening of the way?"

"What does that mean?" I ask. "The opening of the way."

"It means that the gates of Hell itself will open, and all its vile creatures will spring forth into this world." She moves to stand near me and strokes my hair. "Daughter,

for all that my errors cast you into this place, fear not. Use the dagger and let me help you."

"What is the price?" I ask again.

"Malizander feared it, too. You know this," she says.

"Yes."

"And yet she overcame her fears. She lived and was able to hide the Boards. With my aid, she was able to escape Malkander and his minions. Can you say you will be able to do the same—without me?"

"I have lived long enough to know that what my grandfather told me is true. Nothing is free, and if someone doesn't want to tell you the price, it must be high."

Shalizander steps away from me and gazes into my eyes. She is power and love and faith and pain and so much more. She is my mother, the first mother of all the Solitaires. The mother of the Keepers.

"What is the price?" I ask. "What will this aid cost me?"

"The price, my daughter, is your soul," she says. "I must become you."

"No," I whisper. "I . . . I cannot pay that."

"You must," she says. "For I am your only hope of defeating Peraud and Malkander. Go back to the real world, and think on it for a time. But not too long, my daughter. Even now, you struggle to contain the Boards, and even now, Malkander plots against you."

She makes a dismissive gesture with her hand, and I

hear Simon calling me from a great distance, telling me it is time to wake up. Something is happening.

"Think on it, Daughter," Shalizander whispers as I move toward consciousness. "Think on it while you say good-bye to the lost souls of Pompeii. But don't think too long, or all you know and love will be lost."

14

"My Lord—it hurts—it hurts so much. I feel . . . empty and hollow."

"There, there, Peraud. It has been a while since you've felt real pain, hasn't it? You have continued to underestimate young Jenna Solitaire, and this time, the price of your foolishness was quite high. Higher even, than I think you know."

"Please, my Lord—save me. Don't let her have me."

"I'm sorry, Peraud, but you have run out of chances. I have already begun preparing your replacement. The spell of replication has already been accomplished."

"My replacement? No, my Lord! Save me this once more and—"

"See there, Peraud? Death is not so hard, and even I can be moved to a lion's mercy."

"Jenna, wake up," Simon said, shaking me gently. "You've got to see this."

"I'm awake," I said, opening my eyes. "What is it?"

He pointed out the window, and I saw that we were parked near the ruins of Pompeii. The single headlight of the truck illuminated the street, and even from this distance I saw strange flickers of light coming from the central square, where I had confronted the ghosts of the city a few days ago.

"What's going on?" I asked.

"I don't know," he said. "But I have the feeling that we're supposed to be there." He shut off the truck and doused the headlight, bringing the odd flashes into even sharper relief. "Let's go," he said.

I climbed out of the truck and moved to the back. "Bring Amber," I said.

The German shepherd who had been my guardian and companion was sound asleep in the back, if not unconscious. There had been little I could do for her injury before, and I suspected that any veterinarian in this region would simply put her to sleep.

"What for?" Simon asked. "Let her rest."

"She's not just a dog," I said. I quickly explained what I had learned about the spirits of Pompeii and their promise to provide a guardian should a Keeper ever return here. "She's a human soul within a dog. Just like every dog here."

239

Simon shuddered. "That's a form of possession," he said, sounding aghast.

I shrugged. "If it wasn't for her, things might have worked out a lot differently back there," I said. "Let's just be thankful and get this over with, okay?"

He nodded, and gently lifted Amber out of the gate. Other than a soft whine and licking him once on the face, she didn't make a sound, but just looked at me with her unblinking amber eye. I had a pretty good idea what she was thinking, and I hoped that it would happen soon.

With Simon carrying Amber, we made our way to the ruined center square of Pompeii. Once again, it was filled with hundreds of spirits, whirling in a ghostly dance that only they understood the steps to. But as we walked to the edge of the square, the dance suddenly stopped, and a pathway to the center stone opened up.

"Head for the center," I instructed Simon.

He did as I asked, laying Amber down on the stone when we got there. As before, a spirit in flowing robes coalesced more solidly in front of me, and he spoke. *"Keeper, you have returned, and we sense that you carry the destructive Board of the Flames with you."*

"I do," I replied. *"We will be leaving this place tomorrow. The volcano has been returned to its natural state."*

"And you have brought your guardian back," it said.

"Yes," I said. "She was . . . she is wonderful. Who was she, in your time?"

"My wife," he replied solemnly. "She believed in you. I do not like to see her in pain."

"Neither do I," I said. "Yet I thank you for fulfilling the promise made so long ago."

"Now you must fulfill yours," the spirit said. "Leave this place and never return. Only then will our spirits be freed. Tonight, we dance for the last time."

Curious, I asked, "Why do you dance?"

"There is nothing else for us. The dead cannot touch, cannot feel, cannot laugh or cry or do any of the other things that bring life into joy. So we dance as a dim reminder of what once was."

"I understand. What will happen to Amber?"

"The one you call Amber will be released from her pain," it said. "And the spirit of my wife that inhabits her will join us as we move into the next world."

"I understand."

"Leave now, Keeper," it replied, its voice as cold as moonlight. "Or perhaps you wish to dance with us?"

I had a pretty good idea what that meant and shook my head. I stepped over to where Amber was stretched out upon the stone. "Thank you," I said. "For everything."

"Thank you, Keeper, for helping me to fulfill the promise and for earning our release."

A cold tongue appeared and licked me on the chin. "Good-bye, Amber," I whispered.

Then I turned to Simon and said, "We're done here. Let's go."

"Agreed," he said. "There is a coldness of spirit here that I do not like at all."

"They've been trapped here for a long time," I said, heading out of the square and back toward the truck. "Everything comes with a price."

"That's true enough," he said. "I feel like when I was with Peraud's men I really missed out on some things. Can I buy you a late cup of coffee and a sandwich and you can fill me in?"

"Not tonight, Simon," I said, thinking of what I had learned here and what I wished I didn't know. "I just want to rest."

For a moment he looked like he was going to protest again, but he simply nodded and said, "Okay, we'll catch up tomorrow. I could use a good night's sleep myself. Let's get back to the hotel."

We drove the few blocks to the hotel and parked the old truck in the street. The next day, Simon would see to it that it was returned and that Dario's body was recovered and properly laid to rest. He escorted me to my room, and at the door, he paused and said, "Jenna, I want—I need to tell you something."

I looked at him, seeing all the struggles he'd gone through written in his eyes. "What is it, Simon?"

"The last few days . . . ." he started; then his words stopped and he tried again. "Since I've met you. . . ." Once more, his words trailed off into silence.

I didn't press him, because whatever was on his mind was obviously difficult for him to say.

Finally, he said, "Jenna, I . . . I do have feelings for you. I wanted to deny that before, but I can't. I've come to care about you too much to simply dismiss those feelings that easily, no matter what."

My heart took a sudden leap into my throat.

"But," he continued, "I don't know how to protect you any other way than by staying true to my faith. Peraud, I think, is only a shadow of the evil behind him. The Boards themselves gather darkness like nothing else in this world. If I risk turning away from God's will for me, I could put you in more danger, not less."

I nodded, understanding at last that pushing him was not the answer. He would have to work out the conflict on his own. "Simon, I haven't kept my feelings for you secret, and maybe I should have," I said. "I don't necessarily agree with your interpretation of God's will, but that's between you and Him, and not for me to decide. I'll support your decision, so long as you make a promise to me."

"What would that be?" he asked.

"That the next time a bad guy calls you for a meeting, you don't go without me," I said, smiling.

"Deal," he said.

Then he wrapped me in his arms and held me tightly to his chest. I couldn't help it—I put my arms around him as well. For a long minute or two, I was home and so was he—and we both knew it. For whatever reason, we belonged together. That, too, was a destiny. But for now. . . .

Simon stepped away and said, "Good night, Jenna. Rest well."

"Good night, Simon," I said.

I let myself into my room and closed the door behind me. Like a sleepwalker, I moved through the room, shedding my dirty and ruined clothing and leaving it on the floor. I tossed my battered backpack on the bed. I took a bath, soaking for almost an hour before finding the will to lather up and get clean enough to get out of the water. Then, wrapping myself in a towel, I climbed beneath the blankets and stared at the ceiling.

I was afraid to sleep. Shalizander would be waiting for me, eager for my decision. The Boards had been quiet in my head as they talked among themselves, but that would end in time. Already, I could hear their faint whispers in the back of my mind, like three powerful mice plotting behind a wall.

I opened the pack and took out my BlackBerry. When I powered it up, I saw that there were two e-mails waiting for me. I read the first one and was pleased to see a note from Father Andrew that read:

Dear Jenna—

Tom was kind enough to supply me with your e-mail address and phone number. As he told you, I will be coming to Rome for an extended visit with Vatican officials next week. I know that when they hear what I have to say, many of those officials would like to meet you in person, but more importantly, I want to see you.

If you can, please send me an e-mail when you arrive in Rome, and we'll make time to get together. I hope you are safe and well and that Simon is taking care to protect you.

In faith,
Father Andrew

I jotted a quick reply, promising to get in touch when we were there, and asking him to not reveal anything about my role in what happened back home until we could talk about it. Then, I moved on to the next e-mail, which was from Tom.

Dear J.—

I hope you are well and that Father Andrew was able to get in touch, too. This is going to sound crazy, but I'm sending this from a new account and please don't tell Kristen I've been in touch with you. She's . . . I don't know what she's doing, but she's not acting like herself at all.

One day, she talks about how much she misses you and wishes this would all end so you could come home, and then next she's muttering in her sleep about undeserved power and the eye. It's all very strange. I don't know where we go from here, I really don't. Every time I try to talk to her about it, she snaps at me and tells me I'm imagining things or being paranoid.

Did you get the next Board yet? How are things between you and Simon? Tell me what's going on in your world, Jenna, so I don't worry about you 24/7, but can cut it back to 22/7!

Before I forget, there is one thing Kristen and I did find out about your

great-grandmother. She was pregnant *before* she arrived in America, J. And before she was married. It must have been
quite the scandal at the time! If only we
knew who her lover was, we might be able
to find out more.

Guess that's all for now, but I'll be in
touch soon and hope to be able to explain
what's really going on with Kristen.

In the meantime, please, PLEASE take
care of yourself, J. We miss you.

Tom

I drafted a reply, concern for my two best friends a
new burden on my heart. Tom and Kristen were my
lifelines to reality, to home. If something was wrong between them, I didn't know what I would do.

Dear T.—

I don't know what to say. That doesn't
sound like the Kristen I know either.
Please write more to me about it when you
can, and be assured I won't say a word to
her. Also, please be careful. I've
learned that a little (and sometimes a
lot) of paranoia can be a good thing.

I now have the third Board in my possession, and tomorrow we leave for Naples, and then on to Rome. As to your question about my great-grandmother, I found out that her lover and my real great-grandfather was a man named Dario Fidelis. He was a priest long ago and a great man. It was fate, perhaps, that led me here and allowed me to get to know him a little bit before he died.

Once more, I find myself alone in the world. Simon will be my friend, but that is all we can be for now. His faith is too important to him for me to take it away from him.

There is so much more I would like to tell you—the things I have learned here about the true history of the Keepers and how Pompeii was destroyed—but it would take more than I can put down in words right now. My heart is too tired, and too broken.

I have to get some rest, but I'll check in again soon. Take care of yourself and write me as soon as you can.

Love,
Jenna

I shut down the Blackberry, put it away, then turned out the lights. There was no use putting off sleep any longer. My dreams would be there whether I faced them now or in an hour. As my eyes closed, I realized that the Boards were whispering louder, and I wondered what they were up to just as I fell asleep.

Searing towers of flames leap high into the night sky, bright enough to obscure the moon and the stars, jumping and cavorting on pillars of air.

In the center of the inferno, I am dying.

My lungs burn, the searing heat sucking every breath away before it is fully taken. Blinded by tears, deafened by the roar, I know that death is only moments away.

The fire elementals I have summoned with the power of the Board will cavort in the open for a short time before descending on me and devouring me whole.

And still I long for the Board's burning kiss, ache to control it and make it mine once more. . . .

This is the dream I had before, I realize, and I wonder why it is repeating itself.

"Because, Daughter, you failed to see who the dreamer was." Shalizander steps out of the shadows near a tree and waves her hand. The fire elementals cease their capering dance and freeze in place. "The power of dreams,"

she says, "is to instruct, to warn, and to aid. They can be easily manipulated."

"What is the warning of this dream?" I ask as she moves closer.

"Do you know where this is?" she asks, gesturing at the unfamiliar landscape.

"No," I say, shaking my head. "I have never been here."

"This is the land of what is now called Scotland," she says. "You will travel there soon."

"I'm going to Rome," I say. "Something isn't right with the Boards."

She laughs lightly. "Jenna, there are four Boards of the Elements, but you are missing the key. After you visit Rome, you will travel to Scotland to begin your search for the next Board. Only when you have all the pieces will you be able to assemble the master Board."

I look at the landscape, trying to memorize it. "Who is the dreamer?" I ask. "And how did she lose control of the Boards?" I look at the figure kneeling in the burning light. "She is a Keeper. How did she get the Board of the Flames and then return it to Vesuvius?"

"You ask questions, Daughter, when the answers are right there for you to see," Shalizander says.

"What do you mean?" I ask. "I don't understand."

"Daughter, all your dreams are true dreams, yes?"

"Yes," I say.

"Then you need to know that this dream is a warning of what might come, not of what has already happened." Shalizander moves away, her face sad. "This may come to pass. Not all the Keepers are strong enough to bear the burden of one Board, let alone three . . . or more."

"Help me," I say. "Help me to understand."

Shalizander turns and looks at me. "Use the dagger, Daughter, before it's too late."

"Too late for what?"

"To save you," she says, walking back to the shadows at the base of the trees.

"Save me? From whom? From what?"

"Daughter, look closer," she says. "The dreamer is you."

I move toward the cowering figure and see that Shalizander has not lied. I am the dreamer. I have lost control of the Boards and they have deserted me, betrayed me to my death.

I turn to look for Shalizander, to beg for her help, but the shadows have swallowed her whole.

Above me, the elementals begin to spin once more, and the burning heat of their fire consumes me once again.

There is a price for everything, I think as I die in my dream, even for doing nothing at all.

Despite the vividness of the dream, I didn't awaken, but slept the night through. I awoke tired, however, and dragged around my room until it was time to check out.

The next morning, Simon made arrangements for the truck to be returned to the villa and for the Templars to come and recover Dario's body discreetly, for burial in Pompeii. I sat in the café and drank cappuccino and didn't say much. I was too busy thinking about my dream from the night before and what Shalizander had told me. Without her, it seemed that I would lose control of the Boards.

But if I used the dagger, I would lose myself.

When he was finished, he returned to the café and showed me the train tickets that would take us to Naples, and then on to Rome. We ate a quick lunch and made it to the train station, where our car was virtually empty. We sat in silence for quite a while until Simon asked, "Do you want to tell me about it?"

"About what?" I said, still lost in my thoughts.

"Something happened while I was being held by Peraud's men," he said. "You've learned some things, I think, that you didn't like very much. Maybe if we talk about it, I can help."

"I don't even know where to start, Simon," I said.

"Wherever it feels right," he said. "Just pick a place and we'll go from there."

"Dario was my great-grandfather," I whispered.

Simon's eyes widened in shock. "I . . . I'm sorry," he said. "I didn't know."

"How could you?" I asked. "I didn't know for sure myself until after he was dead."

"I was there," Simon said. "Who told you that?"

"Malkander," I said. "When you were unconscious, he showed up to rescue Peraud."

"What do you mean, 'showed up'?" Simon asked. "Malkander was Shalizander's lover. He's been dead for. . . ." He paused and looked at me. "He's not dead?"

"No," I said. "He never was. He's some kind of immortal sorcerer."

"Wonderful," Simon said. "Is there anything else I should know about? The apocalypse starting? Signs from Revelation?"

"There's a lot to talk about," I said. "I've learned more in the past few days than I've had time to process."

"Like what?" Simon asked.

"Like the fact that there are *five* pieces to create the Master Board of the Elements," I said. "Not four."

"What's the fifth piece?" he asked, his usual curiosity coming through. "Once we have the Board of the Earth, they should fit together like a puzzle."

I shook my head. "They don't. There's a fifth piece of

some kind, and we need to figure out what it is and fast."

"It's never been mentioned in any of the materials I've ever read," he said. "There are only four elements."

"There is a fifth element, Keeper," the Board of the Winds hissed. *"The only other constant and what binds the four of us together."*

"What is it?"

"In time, you will understand," it replied, then would say no more.

"The Board of the Winds confirms that there is a fifth element of some kind," I said. "What it is, we'll have to figure out for ourselves."

"Perhaps Armand can offer us some insight in Rome," he said. "But where the Board of the Earth is, I don't know."

"It's north of here, somewhere in Europe," I said. "We'll begin our search in Scotland."

"Scotland?" he asked. "Why there?"

"I'm not sure," I admitted. "But I . . . I dreamed about it."

"It's a place to start, anyway," Simon said. He looked like he wanted to talk more, but then he smiled. "Why don't you try to rest some more? You haven't been getting all that much sleep."

"Thank you," I said, promising him that we would talk more later.

I leaned back against the seat and let the motion of the train lull me. I wasn't going to sleep. Not with Shalizander waiting for an answer. Not to face the dreams again. Soon enough, we'd be in Rome trying to track down the Board of the Earth while figuring out what the key was that bound the four Boards together.

I was going to need Shalizander's help, I realized. Despite my will, the rocking motion of the train began to carry me into sleep. Shalizander's help came at such a very high price. It would mean giving her a permanent place within my mind and my body.

"Yes, Daughter," I heard her whisper. "But think of the power you will wield."

"The power," the Boards said in my mind. "Yes."

"The power to open the way," she said, her voice echoing in my mind. "Or to prevent it from being opened. That is the power you must wield, Daughter. The power to open the way."

EPILOGUE

"She's coming to Rome. I'd like to make sure that when she arrives there are plenty of surprises waiting for her."

"I've already seen to it, my Lord. I am certain that the Keeper will not be prepared for the shadows she finds here. Rome can be a very surprising place to those who don't know its secrets."

The sound echoes through the tunnels, chasing my running footfalls. The sound is that of howling wolves, but having seen my pursuers, I know better.

These are wolves disguised as men. Dark-skinned and dark-eyed, with flowing mustaches and white, embroidered shirts.

My breath comes in short, sharp gasps as I race through the subway tunnels, praying with each breath that I can find a way out a way up before the wolves— or one of the trains—catch up to me.

Behind me, the howls begin to fade, and ahead, a beam of light slants down.

I force myself to move faster. Perhaps it is a manhole cover with a ladder going up. Up into the streets, into the throngs of people where I can disappear, find help, find escape.

I am unsure how I got here, how long I have been running. I do not feel the Boards, cannot call on their aid, and a wave of sorrow passes through me.

The Boards are as lost as I am.

The light is ahead and I skid to a stop, almost falling as I see the metal rungs buried in the concrete. Escape, I think, climbing the stone ledge to the ladder.

I climb upward, moving as fast as I can, though my muscles burn with exertion, my lungs heave with the need for oxygen.

Below me, in the darkness, sounds echo strangely, but I do not hear the wolves. Above me, I can see the grid of the manhole cover, and I reach the top rung. I am exhilarated until I see it . . . The padlock that will keep me from the street above, from safety.

This knowledge does not prevent me from pushing on the manhole cover, shoving my right fist against the cold metal bars with all my strength. In the street above, I can hear voices, cars, the sounds of life.

Life.

"Help! Somebody help me!" I scream, my words a last resort. A plea for life.

The sound of the wolves is coming closer once more, and farther away, the rumble of a subway train on the tracks. I can feel the vibrations in the rungs.

"Anybody? Can anybody hear me?"

I feel the hand wrap around my ankle as a voice, low and sinister, says, "I can, Keeper of the Boards."

I scream, unable to stop myself. From above, there is no answer.

From below, the sharp yank on my leg that pulls me from the ladder and into the darkness below.

I hit the stone ledge, the last of my breath leaving my lungs, pain lancing through my back, my spine.

The voice of the wolf whispers in the dark, "Scream if you want, Keeper. Scream and moan and beg."

Desperate for air, I inhale past the pain. "Why?" I whisper. "Why do you hunt me?"

The wolf laughs, and nearby, I can hear the running feet of his brothers. "For sport, Keeper," he says. "And for money."

"I . . . I can pay you," I say. "I can pay a lot."

"You will, Keeper," he says, leaning closer. The darkness is so complete I cannot see him, only hear his low voice and feel his hot breath on my cheek. "But the coin you'll be paying is flesh and blood."

I scream again as his hands touch me and I feel the

scratch of his long nails, his claws on my skin. The others are here. Howling, laughing, calling out for a taste of my overheated flesh.

"Scream, Keeper," the wolf says. "It makes your blood hotter."

The Boards and Shalizander are gone, and I am a Keeper no more.

I am only a young woman, alone in the dark underground, with the wolves all around. I am just Jenna Solitaire.

And I do what the wolf says.

I scream and scream, and the only answer that comes back to me is the howling of the wolves and the rumble of the coming train.

ACKNOWLEDGMENTS

With continued gratitude to Martin H. Greenberg and Larry Segriff for ensuring that these stories came to light, John Helfers and Susan Chang for editorial guidance and vision, Kerrie Hughes for cleaning up after me, Sherri for helping me earn my fiftieth free Starbucks (that's a *lot* of coffee), and as always, to the four "M's," for everything.

ABOUT THE AUTHOR

Jenna Solitaire was raised in Ohio and now lives the life of a vagabond, searching the world for the next Board. When she was nineteen, she learned that she was the Keeper of the Boards, and her life has been filled with magic and mayhem ever since. With Simon Monk, she continues to travel the world and learn about the Boards of Babylon. She believes that sharing her story with others is important and plans on continuing to do so for as long as she can. Her first two journeys were chronicled in *Keeper of the Winds* and *Keeper of the Waters*. Her next journey is chronicled in *Keeper of the Earth*.

Please visit her website at *www.tor.com/jennasolitaire* for updates about her adventures, to read her blog entries, or to send her an e-mail. She loves hearing from her readers, and she'll try to answer you from wherever she is, if she can.